Advanc

MA...

A HISTORICAL NOVEL

"The book is very interesting and worthwhile reading, containing facts not generally known about life in the 1800s. It describes the turbulent times in Europe resulting in the Mallast family's migration from Germany to America in 1882. The reader participates in decisions and hard work that probably mirror, in many ways, our forefathers' actions in making a rewarding life in America. Farm life in America is described in detail along with various family adventures as they struggle in their new country. Bob has done a great job in charting late nineteenth century history in our great country."

—**Mark T. Hogan,** *Director, Visteon Corp. and former Group Vice President for Advanced Vehicle Development, General Motors*

"Mr. Prevost has captured his family's journey from Germany to the vast opportunities available in America's Midwest, particularly in Michigan. The unsettled times in Germany make the decision to migrate to America and begin farming there very compelling. The author quickly makes you feel part of the family, and you become invested in all their hardships and triumphs."

—**Dennis Hextall,** *President and Commissioner, International Hockey League and former Detroit Red Wings Captain*

MALLAST

A HISTORICAL NOVEL

BOB PREVOST

RLP INDUSTRIES

Harrison Twp, MI

Published by
RLP Industries
Harrison Township, MI

Publisher's Cataloging-in-Publication Data
Prevost, Bob.

    Mallast : a historical novel / Bob Prevost. – Harrison Township, MI
    : RLP Industries, 2012.

    p. ; cm.

    ISBN13: 978-0-9846369-0-7

    I. Title.

    PS3616.A45 M35 2012
    813.6—dc23   2012905121

FIRST EDITION

Project coordination by Jenkins Group, Inc.
www.BookPublishing.com

Cover and interior art by Bob Prevost
Interior design by Brooke Camfield
Cover layout by Yvonne Fetig Roehler

Printed in the United States of America
16 15 14 13 12 • 5 4 3 2 1

CONTENTS

INTRODUCTION

This is a story of my great-grandfather's family, the Mallasts, who lived in Prussia before and after 1870, the formative year that created the German Empire, and their migration to the United States in 1882. The story evolves to include a young Ohioan, who marries the youngest daughter, and their subsequent life in Ohio.

Most of the characters are my ancestors. Their names as well as their birth, marriage, and death dates are all valid, including brides and grooms and the Anthony family of Ohio. The dates and names are based on Prussian, Michigan, and Ohio records, U.S. Census reports, cemetery records, and a tombstone in Ohio.

The U.S. farms and the two family businesses are likewise authentic, as I used Michigan and Ohio deed and mortgage records to substantiate and geographically locate each.

Significant migration information included in the novel is based on ship manifests.

Wedding information is valid and authentic hotel names are used, though details including receptions and lodgings are not accurate.

Authentic names of businesses, trains, and ships are used throughout the U.S. phase. This is done for color and may not be historically accurate.

Family lore is of course used throughout the book, including how the young Ohioan met the Mallast family.

CHAPTER ONE

MALLASTS IN GERMANY

As dawn seeped over the lowlands of central Prussia that morning in 1879, mist rose from the marshlands on the outskirts of the small rural village of Werdum, situated in the Welna River Valley in the eastern part of the newly created German Empire.

The valley was predominantly farmland, although about 40% remained forest. The numerous small lakes and streams flowing into the Welna River eventually made their way to the large Oder River, which discharged into the Baltic Sea, just east of Denmark.

The Mallast tenant farm was cloaked in muted gray as August Mallast quietly rose from bed. Sensitive to his wife's needs, he would let her sleep in a bit before the hubbub of the day began. Rosina was usually awakened during the night to tend to Bertha, their two-year-old daughter and the newest addition to their family of nine, and she was very tired by the end of the day.

The kitchen was still dark, since the sun had not yet risen. August lit a lantern, put some kindling in the fireplace, and struck a flint spark on the crumpled papers beneath the kindling. The papers had been presoaked with kitchen fat from the evening meal and the fire started nicely, warming the kitchen on this cool mid-October morning.

The leaping flames and crackling wood stirred August's memories of the three wars he had fought in. He had been married to Rosina just two years when Prussia, aided by Austria, started a war with Denmark in 1864.

At an earlier age, as a young teenager barely 13, he had witnessed violence in the monarch's squelching of a revolt. The citizens, striving for a republican form of government and various reforms such as lower taxes and pay for service work, had been harshly put down by the military. In addition, he had observed the wounded returning from defeat at the hands of Denmark in 1850.

Yet all that paled, August thought, next to the horrors he had encountered in the Prussian wars of the 1860s.

"Thank God I wasn't killed or maimed. I certainly don't want our sons to experience what I went through," August said out loud to the empty kitchen.

The German Empire, formed in 1871, had emerged on the shoulders of the most powerful state of Prussia. The Prussian military juggernaut was the model for the German Empire's army and was the basis of Prussia's military and political dominance of central Europe during the 1860s.

The Prussian ideology was mirrored in the German Empire's constitution, which dictated mandatory military service for all males at age 21. Even teenagers could join the voluntary army reserve starting at age 17.

August's oldest son, Rudolph, was nearly 18. While Rudolph hadn't joined the reserves, he would have no choice but to join the military in three years.

"How can I avoid this?" August muttered to himself, chilled within in spite of the warm kitchen. "Rudolph has no comprehension of the tragedies of war and will look upon the army as a big, exciting adventure."

August continued talking out loud as he prepared a pot of coffee to help roust the boys, Rudolph and his younger brother Adolph, into action for the morning chores.

His reoccurring war memories and the volatile mid-European political climate nudged his desire to protect his naïve family. Adolph would be 18 when Rudolph was 21; no doubt he would want to share in his big brother's adventure by joining the reserves. Then the goose would be up, August thought, since the reserves, voluntary now, could be activated with the stroke of a pen if Germany got itself into another war.

This was not a comforting thought, especially since some of the newspaper articles were predicting a dire future based on the various volatile and shifting relations with European neighbors. They were portraying the situation as a powder keg, waiting for a burning fuse.

"What can I do?" August continued his one-way conversation as he hung the coffee pot to brew over the blazing fire in the fieldstone fireplace.

Again, he thought of the three wars he'd served in, starting when he was 28: Denmark in 1864, Austria in 1866, and France in 1870–71. He'd had a full eight years of war including training, with short but romantic interruptions between each of the three conflicts. What a way to start married life, he recalled, going off to war leaving his twenty-one year old wife and a baby in the crib. And on top of that, adding more children after each conflict.

He had asked Rosina's parents for her hand just before the wars started. He remembered how surprised and shocked they'd been.

Their initial reaction was not too unexpected by August. "After all," they'd said, "she's only 19!" But after the initial shock wore off, and with more discussion and urging by Rosina, reason prevailed. Fortunately, her parents had finally embraced the plan, and after some time and continued discussions amongst themselves, their concern had turned to joy. In a few weeks, they'd even enthusiastically entered into the wedding planning.

"They even grew fond of me — I think," August chuckled to himself.

He thought back on the wedding as he reached for three coffee mugs on the cabinet shelf and set them on the kitchen table. Rosina's parents had graciously given the young couple a significant wedding gift of 200 marks, the equivalent of a half-year's wages for a farmhand.

And so August reminisced about his wedding day, way back in 1861, when at age 26, he'd wed Rosina Kuhn in their home village of Nawisk, Prussia.

Rosina had soon become pregnant, and their firstborn was only one when August had marched off to war in Denmark. It was 1864 when he'd reported to the Rogasen Regiment, assigned to the 5th Army Corp of the Prussian 3rd Army. Rosina and baby Rudolph had moved in with her parents while he was away fighting.

He had survived the war with Denmark, won easily by Prussia with the help of Austria. Upon his return home, he had moved his wife and son into a small, one-bedroom apartment.

He'd described his war experiences in general terms, not wanting to give his young Rosina the gory details. He recalled his combat at Dybboel Mill, where 5,000 Danes were killed or wounded while 1,000 Prussians and Austrians suffered the same fate.

Rosina's parents had supported her and the baby while August was away, so his savings, along with her parent's very generous wedding gift, put them in a comfortable financial position following the war. Nonetheless, after a short recovery period, August had begun looking for and found work on local farms.

It wasn't too many months after his return from Denmark that Rosina happily told August, and then proudly announced to their parents, that she was expecting another baby.

Their second child was also a boy, three years younger than Rudolph, named Adolph. Soon another war started, this time in the south, against the powerful country of Austria. Austria was considered by many to be a very formidable foe, capable of defeating Prussia, so off August marched again, anticipating a more difficult and lengthy war. He again reported to the Rogesan Regiment, part of the 3rd Army, under the command of Crown Prince Frederick Wilhelm.

Rosina's parents again insisted she move in with them. They knew she would need support in dealing with war news, not to mention help caring for a baby and four-year-old Rudolph.

During his time on the Austrian front, August gave considerable thought to running a tenant farm. He wrote Rosina about his goal. She supported it, and it became their shared dream during and after the war. He also told her they were expecting a major battle at the town of Koniggratz and concluded with, "Pray for me, Rosina."

She prayed nightly and especially hard during Sunday church that August would return safely so they could again move into their own apartment and leisurely enjoy their young family.

"Thank God!" Rosina told her parents when she read August's letter announcing he had survived the battle. He wrote that casualties on both sides had been massive, with 22,000 Austrians killed or wounded while the Prussian armies had suffered 9,000 killed or wounded.

"Rumor has it," he continued in the letter, "that the major Austrian defeat has prompted them to sue for peace. If so, I should be home in the near future."

The war was short — seven weeks in all — and August did return safely. To the surprise of many outsiders, the Prussian army was again victorious. But most important to Rosina, August again returned safely from the southern front, intact and ready to resume their young married life.

Upon his return, they rented a two-room apartment in their village and August set out to find a tenant farm of their own, but he soon found that such opportunities were not in abundance. He had to be content with seasonal work on neighboring tenant farms, but he did not give up on their goal of running a farm of their own, albeit as a tenant.

In spite of this disappointment, Rosina was extremely happy with their married life, so much so that a year after August's return, she was pregnant again.

This time, she delivered twin girls. Her mother moved in with them for a month to help Rosina with the tremendous task of caring for two babies simultaneously plus two other youngsters ages three and six.

August knew at once that their two-bedroom apartment was way too small for his rapidly growing family, especially with his mother-in-law living in. He thought how appropriate it would be if he could somehow convince a landlord to trust him with his farm, especially one with a big farmhouse.

The pieces of life's puzzle seemed to be falling into place, but despite the feeling of destiny at work, August knew it would be a tough sell since he had no experience in running a tenant farm. But he and Rosina had substantial savings, and he hoped this would tip the scales in their favor. He would argue, based on his savings to date, that they could at least pay the first year's rent even if all the crops failed. Plus, he had a number of seasons under his belt working as a farm laborer.

But alas, August again found that getting someone to rent to him was a difficult task. He made his intentions known, and some noblemen owners, knowing he had served in two wars, promised to consider him if their farm should become available.

Perhaps destiny was at work, since only two years after the twins' birth, he was off to war again. If they'd had a farm, Rosina would have been responsible for running it while saddled with four children ages two to eight. An impossibility.

This time, in 1870, August marched west as the German Empire prepared to fend off a French invasion.

It was a turbulent period in German history, one of expansion and consolidation. German Chancellor Otto von Bismarck had orchestrated the war with France under the consenting eye of the Prussian King Wilhelm.

Previously, with von Bismarck at the helm, Prussia, aided by Austria, had easily defeated Denmark. In an ensuing issue with Austria over control of the annexed Demark states, von Bismarck's Prussia declared war on Austria. Much to the surprise of all Europe, the perceived superior Austrian armies were quickly defeated by Prussia. Von Bismarck then organized another German confederation, including the two Denmark states at issue and three northern Germanic states that had been loyal to Austria. This group was called the North German Confederation, and it linked all the Germanic states in the northern tier. Concurrently, he used the Austrian-won leverage to facilitate defense treaties with three southern Germanic states previously under the influence of Austria.

Buoyed by the victory over Austria, von Bismarck saw an opportunity to gain even more territory, this time at the expense of France. Accordingly, he baited France into war by proposing a Prussian prince assume the vacant crown of Spain. He knew France would not stand still for a hostile Germany on its east and a Prussian-run Spain on the west, caught between two hostile countries.

As von Bismarck had predicted, France declared war to counter the threat. This was aided by France's perceived rebuke of Napoleon III by Kaiser Wilhelm. Napoleon III demanded that Kaiser Wilhelm withdraw his support of a Prussian Prince to the throne of Spain.

This time, when August marched off with the Rogesan Regiment, Rosina remained in their apartment, resisting her parent's pleas to move in with them during August's absence. In part, she held firm because she knew her parents would have a very difficult time coping with four young children under their roof.

Plus, she knew something that, for the moment, no one else did. The romantic, tearful days leading up to August's departure had produced yet another Mallast. While August was on the western front, he learned of yet another addition on the way!

He was delighted, and more determined than ever to procure a rental farm. He vowed that if he survived, he would become a tenant farmer.

His letter described a major battle at Sedan. As in Austria, the 3rd Army was well organized and with smart telegraph and railroad usage, was battle ready at the border compared to the over-confident but ill-prepared French 1st Army.

"So much so," he wrote, "that the French army took refuge in the fortress at Metz, now under siege by us."

His letter continued, "To our surprise, Napoleon III, the French President himself, was leading the French 2nd Army to break the Metz siege. But after fierce fighting, we inflicted heavy losses on the French army, now surrounded, and Napoleon surrendered. This effectively ended France's ability to cope with us," he continued, "and we set off to capture Paris."

With Prussia in the lead, helped by three southern Germanic states, the city of Paris was besieged. After the battle at Sedan, France had effectively lost its ability to win the war, though it did drag on into 1871 with minor battles fought with hastily gathered French forces.

August did survive, though he missed the birth of his third son, Emiel, in 1871. Rosina was ecstatic that August had again returned safely. Silently, she said a special prayer of thanks during Sunday church, and together they resumed looking for a farm. August told her the losses at Sedan were great, with 8,000 Germans killed or wounded with French losses twice that.

"How lucky I am," he said. "Hopefully there will be no more wars. But," he told Rosina, "I've said that before."

It was now 1871, they had five children, and August was very anxious to obtain a tenant farm. As luck would have it, during one of his visits to the local beer garden to catch up on the news, August heard of a farm whose owner might consider renting. The current tenant wanted to move to the local village to live in retirement.

"See Rosina, it pays to stay abreast of local news at the garden," August told his wife.

Next day, he visited the owner, a local nobleman, whose farm was located in the vicinity of a village called Werdum about six miles away.

The owner of the farm expressed some interest in August's proposal, so August and Rosina traveled to Werdum the next weekend to discuss the possibility of renting in more depth. The nobleman knew his tenant was interested in retiring from farm work, but was reluctant to seriously consider August since he had no experience in running a farm.

August persisted, and after a few visits in which he urged the owner to think about it, he perceived the man was starting to warm up to the idea.

"Why not?" he finally told August. "You fought in the wars and my tenant wants to leave so I'll give you a chance. But you'll have to make payments on time or I'll take the farm back," the nobleman emphasized.

August had tipped the scales, as he'd imagined he might, by sharing the amount of their savings. Sure enough, the owner was reassured that August could make the monthly payments for some time, even if the Mallasts turned out to be lousy farmers. Their savings would give them a few years to get their feet on the ground, and if they couldn't make the payments by then, the owner would seek a new tenant. It was a good business proposition for both sides, and both were happy with the agreement.

The small village of Werdum, like Rosina's parents' village of Nawisk, was a satellite village to the much larger town of Rogasen. Rogasen sat midway between the two villages, each about four miles away. Its population was about 4,000 people, while each of the villages' was about 200. Rogasen, equivalent of a county seat, was home to the civil records office, the police, and the court along with the German Evangelical church for the surrounding area.

The farm itself sat midway between Berlin and the Russian Empire's state of Poland, about 150 miles from each, in the county of Obornik, District of Posen, in the dominant State of Prussia, part of the German Empire of the 1870s.

With their tenant status finally assured, the young couple had a handsome start in life: they were on their own with five healthy children, independent of their parents for financial support, working a tenant farm, with enough money to avoid scrimping to make the monthly payments. The payments were reasonable, and they correctly thought the rent could be earned by tilling the soil with cash crops such as wheat, oats and rye.

The medium-sized 30-acre tenant farm came with six cows and two horses per August and Rosina's agreement with the owner. This allowed August to concentrate immediately on growing field crops without having to re-stock animals and poultry. The river valley soil around Werdum was somewhat sandy, which was not the best for farming, but it was adequate for rye, oats, corn, and marginal for wheat.

August decided to alternate the field crops with hay, one field each year, in an attempt to keep the soil fertile. He also alternated the field crops with some corn, flax, and barley. In addition to crop rotation, August fertilized the fields during winter with manure accumulated during daily barn and weekly chicken coup cleanings.

The manure spreading, crop rotation, and alternating hay fields did indeed keep the fields fertile, which made for good harvests. The sale of grain alone was almost enough to make the monthly payments, while their income from selling milk, cheese from unsold milk, and eggs, along with chickens and geese to meat markets in Rogasen, proved sufficient to supply the rest. They even had some money left over for savings.

The family lived frugally and depended on their farm as much as possible for their own subsistence. Vegetables from their large garden, chicken and duck eggs, fresh milk, poultry for Sunday dinner, some pigs for pork, a heifer for beef and a calf for veal all provided good homegrown food.

They needed such food, for farm work was hard. A horse-drawn plow tilled the fields, seed was sown by hand, grains were harvested with a scythe, and kernels were separated by beating and tossing. This labor-intensive work limited how much acreage one family could handle, and 30 acres was about the limit.

The small nearby village of Werdum contained a few shops servicing the surrounding farms. In addition to a market selling sausage, flour, and local vegetables, fruit, and other food staples, there was a blacksmith and woodworking shop for shoeing horses and repairing farm equipment, a carpenter shop, a beer garden (a very popular gathering place), a small post office, and a one-room schoolhouse.

August realized at once he needed help with the farm and was able to hire a young farmhand in the nearby village. His oldest sons, at nine and six years of age, were too young to be of much help except for lesser tasks such as feeding chickens and pigs, but the hired man helped with multiple tasks: plowing and planting the field crops in late spring, cutting and raking hay into rows for drying, hauling the dried hay into the barn before it rained and became damp, and the labor intensive harvesting of the field crops in late summer and well into the fall.

This work, in addition to hoeing the large garden and helping with the nightly milking, kept the hired hand and the Mallasts very busy. There was plenty to do for a hired man except in winter and early spring, but August made as much work as possible during the slow months. The hired hand repaired equipment and sharpened cutting tools, did carpenter work on the barn, house, and chicken coops, repaired wood rail fences, shoveled the cow manure from the barn, and periodically, during the winter, spread it on the fields. The milking, of course, continued year around.

With the hired man's help, August and the boys soon had the farm bustling. As two more years ticked by, the two boys were helping more and more. To August's relief, their operational plan appeared to be working.

Besides the busy daily farm work, August and Rosina somehow found time and energy to lovingly raise their family and even increase its size by two additional children, Frederick and Bertha, bringing the total number to seven children.

Consistent with the practice of nineteenth century farmers, a large family was almost a necessity if the farm was to be profitable and grow. The young married couple must have sensed they would own or run a farm since they had a good start with that practice even before becoming tenant farmers. The family grew, in German precision, with a birth every three years, starting a year after the wedding in 1861. This practice continued uninterrupted, despite the wars, until 1877, with the birth of their seventh and final child.

In 1879, the first two children, Rudolph and Adolph, now 17 and 14, were handling some of the hard manual farm work, which meant a hired hand was no longer necessary. Emiel and Fred, only eight and five, also had their assigned duties. They worked as a team doing lesser tasks such as bringing the cows in from pasture each afternoon for milking, hoeing in the garden, and gathering eggs. They also mischievously chased the chickens and geese around the farmyard, an unassigned task. Rudolph and Adolph were charged with keeping the younger boys in line, but it was a difficult job.

The industrious, hard-working Rosina kept herself busy from morning to night, caring for and raising the children and tending to the household duties. She was appreciative that eleven-year-old twins Emielie and Adolfine were able to help more and more with the daily household chores.

Things were going well as the children's minds and bodies grew. They were handsome children, and their parents were proud to see them pitch in and help with only minor grumbling and half-hearted efforts to shift jobs to their siblings. Their tenant farm savings increased, helped by the increasing appetite for field crops in the growing German cities, which resulted in good crop prices. Being able to keep farm expenses to a minimum by the use of family labor and frugal family living were also important factors in growing their rainy day savings. These savings would turn out to be crucial as their lives took various major turns in the not-too-distant future.

Such was the comfortable living that August and Rosina Mallast had made for themselves in Prussia as the 1870s gave way to a decade of changes. The farm work was hard, but it provided a comfortable lifestyle. Likewise, the family was healthy and growing nicely. Like all parents, the Mallasts loved their children very much, but trouble was brewing.

CHAPTER TWO

Trouble Brewing

August put another log on the nicely burning fire and removed the freshly brewed coffee from the fireplace hanger. He trudged up the stairs to the landing, heading to the older boys' room to awaken them for the morning chores.

He paused in the hall, looking at his sleeping sons through the open doorway. It would take some firm shoulder shaking to arouse them today.

Before it commenced, August thought again of the war potential. He knew firsthand that Prussia would use its military might aggressively to achieve its political objectives. Consequently, he followed the political maneuverings carefully, well aware that it was the brilliant Chancellor Otto von Bismarck who had orchestrated the growth of the German unions by initiating the three wars he had fought in.

Denmark had been defeated easily by the powerful Prussian Army, with some help from Austria. As a result of the war, two Denmark states at issue, Schleswig and Holstein, were ceded to Prussia and Austria. Von Bismarck wanted to further consolidate the Germanic states and grow the confederation by including both Schleswig and Holstein but Austria balked, as did other members of the confederation.

Shortly thereafter, in 1866, Prussia withdrew from the German Confederation and declared war on Austria over this issue. Although Prussia was very strong, most European countries considered Austria, not Prussia, to be the dominant state in the region.

The powerful Prussian army was victorious, to the surprise of many other countries but not to the Chancellor. The Prussian prize of victory was annexing both former Denmark states, Schleswig and Holstein, into the Prussian-led German Confederation. In addition, Prussia annexed three additional northern Germanic states that sided with Austria in the war, Hanover, Hesse, and Nassau plus the independent city of Frankfurt. These states, although near neighbors of Prussia, had previously been under strong Austrian influence.

The addition of the five states gave von Bismarck control of the entire northern tier of Germanic states and much prestige in Europe. This consolidation was called the North German Confederation, and it nearly doubled the size of the original German Confederation.

Subsequently, von Bismarck was able to grow the North German Confederation even more by another diplomatic ploy. He cleverly maneuvered France into starting a war, thereby triggering Prussian joint defense treaties with southern Germanic states. To the surprise of France, which thought the southern states to be neutral, Baden, Bavaria, and Wurttemburg were pulled into the conflict on the side of Prussia. Von Bismarck believed the Prussian-led German army could easily defeat the French forces, especially with the help of the recently allied three states to Prussia's south.

His scheme was as follows: the throne of France's western neighbor, Spain, was vacant at the time, waiting to be filled by a suitable monarch. Germany, of course, was the dominant neighbor to the east, sharing most of France's eastern border.

Von Bismarck proposed a Prussian prince assume the vacant throne of Spain. He reasoned, correctly, that France and Napoleon III would not stand still if surrounded by Prussian-controlled countries on its two major land borders. This he believed would bring his scheme to fruition and entice France into initiating a war with the Prussian-led German Confederation. Simultaneously, putting Prussia on the defensive would trigger the newly negotiated and somewhat little known joint Prussian defense treaties. France took the bait and invaded Germany over the proposed move in Spain, plus being leery of a powerful consolidated Germany.

Napoleon III ordered the invasion of Germany in July of 1870. His troops crossed the Saar River and seized the town of Saarbrucken, but Chancellor von Bismarck was right again: the French army was easily defeated. Prussia and her allies claimed their spoils of war and annexed most of Alsace and the Moselle part of Lorraine. This region, one of the most important industrial-mineral rich areas in France, now belonged to the newly formed German Empire.

So in the three consecutive wars from 1864 to 1871, von Bismarck was able to grow the unification of German states into a Northern German Confederation, then expand it by including the three defense-treaty southern states into a group called the German Empire. And, importantly, he successfully excluded the previously influential Austria from German affairs.

Von Bismarck was certainly the most dominant person in central Europe during the 1870s, controlling both domestic and military affairs with the concurrence of the Prussian King, Kaiser Wilhelm I. However, the central European political scene during that period continued to be in a constant state of flux. Von Bismarck recognized that maintaining a strong army was vital to the existence of the German Empire, since it was surrounded by less than friendly neighbors.

August understood all this, so he was not surprised that the constitution of the newly formed German Empire mirrored that of the dominant Prussian state and required all twenty-one year old males to enter the military while teenage boys, starting at seventeen, could join the army reserves.

During the 1870s, France continued to seethe over the loss of the mineral-rich states of Alsace and Lorraine. The weekly Rogasen newspaper kept August abreast of the ever-changing situation.

As the months and years passed, August closely followed the Chancellor's chess playing with Russia and France. Making matters more complex, the countries to the south of Austria-Hungary were entering the equation. This multicultural group of Moors and Slavs lived side-by-side in a conglomerate of states between the Adriatic Sea, Russia, Turkey, Austria-Hungary, and the Mediterranean Sea.

The Slavic peoples had deep Russian roots, so Russia felt the protective responsibility of being a big brother. In a similar manner, the Moors associated with the Ottoman Empire. Turkey was a strong country in the Ottoman Empire and felt a responsibility for the Moors of the region. A long history of conflict between these two groups preceded the 1870s. Also, Austria-Hungary still had influence in the Ottoman- controlled countries to its south.

The area was a melting pot of multiple interests, but the citizens all shared a common goal: independence from the powerful states of Austria-Hungary and Turkey. Various revolutions in the late 1870s were crushed, sometimes savagely.

Russia had an influential, big brother relationship with the Slavs and was very upset with the severe treatment in the squelching of the revolution by Austria. Russia was ready to go to war with Austria over this matter. The Russian threat to Austria was squelched by von Bismarck, who made it known the German Empire would fight on the side of Austria if invaded. Not wanting to test the might of the Prussian-led German Empire, Russia instead declared war on Turkey. This seemed safe to Russia, especially since von Bismarck had stated that the German Empire had no interest in the Ottoman Empire or its people.

Russia won the war against Turkey and took as its spoils much more territory for its quasi-state of Bulgaria, even though Russia had promised Austria-Hungary it would not create a large Russian satellite state in this region, commonly called the Balkans. A much larger state of Bulgaria, under Russia's wing, resulted.

Austria wanted to maintain the status quo and was unhappy. Austria did not want to lose influence in the Balkans and strongly opposed Russia's move.

Thus entered the German Empire's Chancellor Otto von Bismarck to settle the disagreement.

Von Bismarck organized a meeting, held in Berlin, to negotiate a settlement. In essence, the meeting decided who would receive any spoils of war. A capital idea, but it was soon discovered by the victorious Russians that even though they had won the war, they did not receive any of the spoils!

The Russian negotiators were livid. It was blatantly obvious that Germany, as if by pre-arrangement, was siding with Austria on every issue, large and small. The Russian negotiators complained vehemently to their king, the Czar. The Czar in turn complained to the German king, the Kaiser, but to no avail. The German Chancellor was in the driver's seat, and the map of central Europe was again re-drawn while Russia fumed. In spite of winning the war, Russia had nothing to show for it except the Slav peoples' perception of a protective big brother. Lacking sufficient political clout, Russia couldn't make her acquisition plans stick. Smoldering, Russia contemplated her next move.

The latest Rogasen weekly newspaper, in 1879, reported the Kaiser had called an urgent meeting with the Chancellor and the Chancellor's military staff to discuss possible hostile actions by Russia. The Kaiser and Chancellor were fearful of a major Russian offensive along the eastern border of Germany, accompanied by a coordinated attack on the western border by France.

The newspaper speculated that for Germany to be ready to repel an invasion, she would need to beef up the already strong German army. This fanned the flames and again presented the situation as a powder keg waiting for a spark. Naturally, August believed Germany was preparing for war.

The Rogasen newspaper confirmed, as feared by the Kaiser and Chancellor, that a Russian army was poised on Germany's eastern border, in the Russian state of Poland. The probable invasion route would be to strike for Berlin, nearly directly in line with the farm. Poland was only 150 miles away.

In addition to the friction with Russia, in the back of August's mind was the memory that four years earlier, France had increased her army size by 25%. The Rogasen newspaper had reported the French army's increase as well as the Empire's reaction. The German army staff interpreted this as hostile action by France, enabling the military to precipitate high-level discussions within the Empire to consider strategies, one of which, reportedly, was initiating an invasion of France!

Von Bismarck and company knew France was bristling over its loss of the prized Alsace-Lorraine industrial region and would jump at the chance to regain it. Perhaps France would again initiate an invasion, but this time in concert with a French ally that had a bone to pick with Germany. France might invade Germany and persuade Russia to join in a coordinated attack, forcing Germany to fight simultaneously on two fronts, both west and east borders.

The Rogasen news reported that relations with Russia had reached a dangerous level. August followed the reports carefully. He made weekly trips to the village beer garden and discussed his opinions with others. Many shared his views and hoped there would be no war, since they had family members who had served in one or more of the wars of the 1860s, some quite tragically.

August's thoughts had wandered far from the farm and the need to do the morning chores. Suddenly returning to the present, he moved into the sleeping boys' bedroom and shook their shoulders, rousing them to action.

"Is it time to get up already?" Adolph groggily asked.

"Yes, Adolph. As you know, the cows need milking before breakfast, and after breakfast, there is still standing corn in the east field that needs to be cut, tied into bundles, and stacked for later husking."

The boys were a big help, reflected August, watching them lumber sleepily to their feet. He would miss them greatly if they entered the army.

After they'd each gulped down a cup of strong coffee, the threesome headed for the barnyard and their six cows.

The milking didn't take too long with only two cows apiece. It was getting the cows into the barn, into their stanchions, cleaning the manure from the barn floor, putting the fresh milk into cans, and then the cans into cold water to cool that took all the time.

Two hours passed quickly. By the time the men had completed the early morning chores, Rosina, with the twin girls' help, had made a hearty breakfast to go with the fresh milk — sausages and freshly baked biscuits, homemade butter, and farm field honey.

After breakfast, the older boys were off to Rogasen to sell the fresh milk and some eggs gathered from the chicken coop while August headed for the cornfield with his scythe and file, ready to start the day's cutting. Repeatedly sharpening the scythe made the cutting easier, but he would leave the bundling, tying, and stacking to the boys to conserve his back and knees. Their younger bodies could more easily take the constant bending needed for the job.

As the sun approached midday, Rudolph and Adolph were sighted with the horse and wagon returning from Rogasen. August headed to the house for a late lunch and to learn of the morning sales. He recorded the day's sales and stashed the coins in a moneybox hidden behind some books neatly placed on a cupboard shelf, ready for the month's rent payment.

The milk was nearly all sold and the twin girls would churn the remainder into butter while the unsold eggs would be a good treat for tomorrow's breakfast. Or maybe Rosina would make dumplings for Sunday dinner.

After lunch, the threesome walked to the cornfield.

"Rudolph, do you miss attending school in the village?" August suddenly asked his oldest son.

Rudolph, who had recently completed school, said, "Yes, I do miss seeing my schoolmates on a daily basis."

August continued, "Perhaps you could check on some of the activities at our church in Rogasen. Aren't some of your friends active there?"

"Yes, Father, you're right, but the beer garden might be good as well," countered Rudolph mischievously.

August smiled back. What a shame, he thought, if these healthy, fun-loving boys should be required to fight on the front lines and perhaps be maimed or even die.

He again thought of the growing unrest. Von Bismarck had set about forming a three-way alliance with Russia and Austria-Hungary and also a separate alliance with France. He did not want Russia and France to become friendly for fear of a coordinated attack on two fronts. Unfortunately, the Russian alliance hadn't worked for long since Austria and Russia had different objectives for the Balkan states.

August concluded that two wars were a real possibility. Russia was very angry over losing the anticipated spoils of war with Turkey and over Austria-Hungary's treatment of the Slavic people in their quasi-southern states, and France was very angry over its loss and was looking to regain the Alsace-Lorraine region.

No doubt about it; his sons would be inducted into the army, perhaps even at an earlier age than 21, and surely would be engaged in frontline warfare. In fact, they would probably be the first to volunteer for what they would perceive as a great adventure.

It would indeed be a great adventure, but it would soon turn into something they hadn't bargained for.

So in spite of feeling satisfied with their life in Werdum, a troubled August felt a real concern that he needed to share with Rosina in the near future.

"What to do?" he said aloud to Wolfgang, his favorite horse, as he fed him a fresh carrot. Perhaps he should seriously consider a bold move, even leave Germany entirely.

"This sounds drastic," August thought to himself, "until you consider the potential cost of staying — the lives of our beloved sons."

CHAPTER THREE

The Decision

The tenant farm, nestled snugly in the northeast corner of Prussia, provided the young Mallast family with a comfortable living. August and Rosina had both grown up in the surrounding countryside, and they both had deep roots.

Their garden plantings increased as did their poultry flocks, all possible since the growing children were able to carry more and more of the workload. This, along with intelligent crop decisions, resulted in their farm income increasing a little each year. In turn, the farm payments were made on time, every time. The farm was hard, healthy work but it provided a very comfortable lifestyle.

Life was too good, thought August. He had an inner feeling something bad was bound to happen. His feeling was not without some merit, as the Rogasen weekly newspaper continued to publish troubling reports regarding the German Empire's relations with neighboring countries. Germany, the newspaper reported, was headed for a confrontation with neighboring France and possibly even the big country of Russia to the east.

"Maybe there are storm clouds ahead," he said out loud as he fed some oats to Wolfgang, their gelding carriage horse and main means of transportation and shopping in the nearby village of Werdum.

August became more and more concerned as time went on and the newspaper continued the coverage of deteriorating relations with Germany's neighbors. August read the news with a twinge of concern and apprehension. He believed an army buildup would occur, perhaps even lowering the required draft age from 21 to the army reserve entry age of 17. Their oldest sons, teenagers Rudolph and Adolph, would surely be inducted into the army, especially if things went badly for Germany.

So despite the feeling of self-satisfaction, a troubled August felt a real concern that he would not yet share with Rosina.

He read that the Kaiser and Chancellor had an urgent meeting with their ministers to discuss possible hostile actions by Russia. Reportedly, the Russian Czar was preparing his armies to invade Austria with a possibility that Germany was also on the list. Russia had reportedly amassed an army in the Russian state of Poland, on the German eastern border, which put Prussia and Berlin itself in the path of a potential invasion.

In addition, France was making repeated statements about ownership of the mineral rich Alsace-Lorraine region, annexed by the Prussian led German Empire following the 1870 Franco-German war.

August's strong concern continued for days after. "What do I do?" he thought as he headed to the stable. "Do we stay and endure the possible future treacherous wars with our sons' lives at risk?"

With two possible conflicts ahead, military action within Germany was indeed likely, perhaps even within the next few years. August knew such action, with the associated loss of life, would be devastating to many families, perhaps even his own. He did not want his children to fight in a war and possibly die on a battlefield. "What can I do to avoid a possible tragic life-ending experience?" August said to his confidant Wolfgang.

He knew his sons would initially look forward to a perceived glorious adventure with the army, especially since many of their young friends would be part of the big build-up as well. After all, they were both healthy and active young men but still in their late teens.

He knew his arguments would not be persuasive against their youthful exuberance. Perhaps they could be delayed a year or so, but if the German government required teenage boys to serve in the Army, they would have to do so. He knew the boys would be drafted and could not avoid being at high risk of death at a very young age. August felt the need to protect their sons, as well as Rosina, from the tragedies of war, which he had witnessed first hand. He knew it would be devastating to Rosina if one or both were killed.

Why was it, August mused, that wars in Europe somehow always involved Germany? Should they stay in Germany anyway and endure these possible future wars?

The loyalty he felt for his country versus his desire to protect his family caused him tremendous conflict.

"I cannot separate the family by sending the boys to another country," he spoke out loud. "Besides, what European country would be safe from possible war? And how would we start a new life with the family in a new country? How would we manage?" He gently patted his horse on the nose.

"Oh Wolfgang," he sighed, "in spite of my fears, how could I possibly leave you and our beloved farm?"

As the weeks passed, August continued to worry. As he did, his resolve grew, and a plan slowly evolved in his thoughtful brain.

He had heard reports in the village of a local family that had migrated to the North America continent, across the Atlantic. He had heard they were doing all right, although they weren't a farming family. They had settled in the Midwestern part of the United States in a region called Michigan.

August needed to learn more. He decided to ask the local relatives if they knew more about this family's situation in America; maybe he would even write to them for more specifics. That would be relatively easy, and the information could be of aid in discussing such a major life-changing decision with Rosina. She was close to her parents, and he knew she would not want to leave Germany.

During his next trip to town, August obtained the information he needed from a man related to the immigrant family, including an address in America. He wrote a letter, deliberately avoiding Rosina's scrutiny by working late at night.

The following week, during their weekly supply trip to the village, he mailed the letter without Rosina's knowledge. Now, all he had to do was await the reply.

August was seeking answers to his questions about any military draft situation in North America, the cost of passage across the Atlantic, details on how to travel once in North America, the cost of travel from the coast to Michigan, and generally what life was like in Michigan including work and farming opportunities. This was a lot to ask, but he wanted as much information as he could get.

August thought the Woltmans would receive his letter in about a month and would answer promptly. He certainly hoped so. Who knew how much time he had before things erupted in Europe?

Time passed, and each week, August volunteered to pick up the mail during their trip to town. Typically, Adolph or Rudolph kept watch over the younger children while Rosina accompanied August and shopped for material, clothes, and other household items. These weekly trips gave August the chance to check the mail without Rosina noticing a letter from North America, and it gave her a break from her hard-working routine and daily farm life.

Seven weeks passed with no letter. Finally, August composed a second, more assertive letter in which he urgently requested information. He also began asking about other people in neighboring villages who might also have made such a move. He was about to follow up on those leads when the reply, after some 10 weeks of waiting, finally came from the Woltmans.

August read the letter with trepidation, but was put at ease after the first few paragraphs. No, the Woltmans wrote, the United States did not have a draft in place, nor was there any talk of war. Further, having crossed the ocean, they knew firsthand how isolated North America was from Europe. The Atlantic Ocean would likely isolate the United States from any war in Europe. And yes, life was good in Michigan, with lots of land and opportunities to pursue farming without high taxes or the need to support centuries-old hierarchies. The Woltmans, in fact, painted a glowing picture of their new homeland. Truth be told, they were pleased that August was considering migrating with his family to North America. This, in their minds, fortified their own decision to leave Germany.

Heinrich Woltman went on to describe fertile soil and good work possibilities, but more importantly, even as a handyman carpenter, he made it clear his family was doing well. Their town, Mount Clemens, was situated on a slight rise adjacent to a river. It had a railroad, creamery, hardware store, bank, blacksmith, livery and clothing and food stores. Oh yes, it even had a beer garden. This gathering spot to share information, he wrote, was called a "saloon" in Michigan.

Heinrich's description continued. A river ran through town, flowing into a lake some seven miles to the east, called Lake St. Clair. The town was located on a slight hill about 20 feet in elevation. Most believe this "mountain" was part of the city's name, given by the first settler on the high bank of the Huron River, Christian Clemens. Clemens had done survey work and laid out lots and streets and had named the future village after himself while incorporating the "mountain" in the name as well. He built his riverside home in the late 1700s and platted the future village in 1818. As far as other "mountains," the countryside east was a delta into Lake St. Clair.

"Relatively flat land with rich soil; ideal for farming," thought August after reading this description.

The letter satisfied his questions about conditions in the United States, and he decided that migrating to America was the best solution. Nonetheless, the move would be life changing, and he wanted Rosina's input and approval.

He considered the best time to break the news to her. Early morning, following a good night's sleep? No, she was too sharp and anxious to begin work at that time. Sunday afternoon, following a church sermon? No — she would be full of news she had discussed with her mother and father after attending the church in Rogasen, and the closeness to her family roots would make the task even harder. Maybe the next alarming newspaper report? Yes, that coupled with past news articles he would save for such a discussion would do it.

The next alarming newspaper report came rather quickly, speculating about a disagreement between Kaiser Wilhelm and Chancellor von Bismarck that had warlike ramifications. The Russian army was on the eastern border and the Chancellor wanted Austria on their side should Russia invade. But Kaiser Wilhelm was fearful an alliance with Austria-Hungary would encourage France to join with the Russians against Germany.

August seized the opportunity to discuss the news with Rosina, stressing the prospect of war on the horizon.

Rosina listened intently, but August knew she was not seriously alarmed yet.

Later that year, in the fall of 1879, von Bismarck did attempt to enter into an alliance with Austria-Hungary against Russia and France. However, Hungary opposed including France in the alliance and got its way. Germany could be assured Austria-Hungary would fight with Germany against Russia, but the Germany Empire would have to fight a war against France on its own.

Now was the time, thought August. He read the news to Rosina, pointing out the great political unrest.

Her reaction was immediate and as expected — a definite "No!" She did not want to leave her comfortable home and beloved farm and did not want to be separated from her parents by an ocean. Living in separate villages eight miles apart was bad enough.

The discussion was heated, and August tactfully withdrew to fight another day.

"Let time do its work," August said to Wolfgang as he fed him a carrot.

Nonetheless, he kept bringing the subject up as often as he dared, trying to keep Rosina open-minded without becoming furious.

Nonetheless, the international intrigue continued with reports that Italy wanted to join with Austria against France. Again August presented his case and kept at it as opportunities presented themselves until Rosina finally began to be persuaded.

Remembering her marriage vows, she grudgingly recalled a phrase "for better or worse," and she finally admitted to herself that August was acting in the best interests of the family. She certainly did not relish the thought of her boys putting their lives on the line in ground battles with Russia or France.

Finally, she agreed to migrate to North America, giving up a comfortable lifestyle and, most importantly, her close association with her parents. She might never see them again, she thought, and what of traveling with four-year-old Bertha?

Obtaining money for such a major step was next. August pondered each step, silently sitting by the comfortable fireplace, logs aglow, late into the evenings, thinking, puffing away on his long, skinny pipe, while Rosina and the family slept.

He composed yet a third letter to the Woltmans in the United States, probing for even more specific information. What was the cost of such a major journey? Could they even afford it? What official papers were needed to leave Germany? Where would he find an ocean-going ship? How many weeks to cross the Atlantic Ocean, and what city was the destination port?

What about lodging upon arrival, and traveling from the ocean port to Michigan?

Finally, would the Woltmans help in making temporary arrangements for lodging and food once they arrived? Would they also inquire about possible farms that could be rented in the surrounding countryside?

More letters followed. Encouraging information flowed to August, especially that the United States government encouraged immigrants since they would help populate the vast country and build up commerce.

Based on the Woltman's information, August thought their savings would pay for their ship passage to America, but they would need to travel in the economy section, called the "steerage" class. The Woltmans warned that traveling in first class was very expensive. Even second class, next above steerage, would increase the ticket price from about 140 marks for one adult to around 240 marks.

Clearly, August concluded, they would need to travel in steerage. Even so, the total would be over 600 marks — more than two or three years' farm profits!

On top of that, the conditions in steerage did not sound good. August thought Rosina could endure them, but what of the three young children, especially Bertha?

This wouldn't be a pleasant adventure. The living arrangements in steerage might by too rough for the young girls, possibly even for Rosina, and August wasn't willing to commit to traveling in the steerage area without some assurance it would be tolerable for weeks on end.

"What to do now?" August spoke out loud, as was his habit.

It was late in 1881. Rudolph was fast approaching 21, so there was not much time left. Once he joined the army, he would not be allowed to leave without completing his military service.

August decided then and there to send his two teenage sons, Rudolph and Adolph, to experience firsthand the journey in steerage class, assuming they were allowed to migrate from Germany. They would check out shipboard living conditions and mail their report back upon arrival in America. August would still have some options if they thought the conditions would be unbearable for their younger siblings. He also decided not to tell anyone, even Rosina, of his plan until he knew more about the approval process for migrating from Germany, especially for young men.

He inquired at the Civil Records Office in Rogasen during his next trip to the village. The Records Office advised that military approval was necessary for men over 21 to leave Germany. He was very happy to learn no approval was required for younger males. He had feared the allowable age would correspond to the military reserve age of 17.

"Wolfgang, I think it is the only answer, but I will miss the farm and my favorite horse," August said as he patted the gelding's neck. "I need to have the boys travel to America as soon as possible, in steerage, and write back at once about the conditions. They know their siblings' tolerance to trying situations; after all, they have played tricks and teased them enough to know what they can endure short of crying. They will need to predict if the conditions will be bearable for Rosina and the children."

"They will need to write as soon as they arrive in America," he told Wolfgang, "even prior to their arrival, in case they can send the letter back on the return voyage of the ship. Once their letter is received, I will have to decide if the family can endure steerage quarters for two or three weeks' time. If not," he sighed, shaking his head, "we might have to split up the family. Before I do that, I will ask for a loan from my parents, and probably also Rosina's parents, to afford a second-class cabin for my delicate ones. The younger boys will just have to travel in steerage with me. Yes, that will do," he concluded.

August and Rosina broke the news first to their children and then to their parents. Their parents were very sad of course — they realized they would probably never see their children and their beloved grandchildren again!

The following day, August hitched Wolfgang to their small carriage and traveled the four miles to Rogasen, where he obtained and filed the necessary migration papers with the German government. He wrote the necessary letter on the spot, stating the boys had permission to travel without their parents and had it officially stamped by the Civil Records Office in Rogasen. But he was unable to obtain information about ship passage. He did learn that ship passage information could be obtained in the much larger city of Posen, some 24 miles away.

August set out early next morning with Wolfgang hitched to the carriage. He arrived at Posen in early afternoon and was successful in obtaining some information, including addresses for immigration ship offices in the North Sea ports of Hamburg and Bremerhaven. He was told these were the major ports for migration departures by sea.

Then and only then did August tell Rosina of the plan to send their sixteen- and nineteen-year-old sons, by themselves, to assess the travel conditions aboard a ship packed with hundreds of migrating families.

As he had guessed, Rosina did not want to split the family up, but unable to successfully argue against August's logic, she reluctantly agreed.

Letters to and from the ship offices in Hamburg and Bremerhaven followed, giving specific information about estimated ship departure dates and initial payment requirements.

August found the Port of Bremerhaven had a ship, the SS *Oder*, leaving in May. It was now early 1882, and August had to move fast.

He told Rudolph and Adolph the plan, wondering as he spoke how they would react to such important news and the adventure of a lifetime. After all, their departure was set for May, only two months away, and he had already reserved two spaces in steerage for them.

Initially, the boys were shocked and apprehensive about such a big adventure, especially the thought of being on their own for a few months in America. Their immediate reaction gradually gave way to mild enthusiasm, and after a few days, they started to look forward to it, especially the part about being on their own for a while.

"No more farm chores and field work — we can just sit back and enjoy the voyage and city life in the Port of New York," Rudolph told his younger brother.

August was told at the ship ticket office in Posen that his sons would be checked for health and would need to successfully answer some key questions before being allowed to enter the United States. The agent said the United States wanted to be assured the immigrants had an occupation, what it was, who their contact was in the United States, their destination address, and to make sure they had enough money in their pockets to tide them over until they found a job.

This took August aback. He knew both boys were healthy and could use the Woltman's address as contact and destination, but the question of occupation was of concern. He envisioned the boys being rejected since they were traveling alone with only farm labor experience and no farm to work on in America.

"What if they won't let the boys into the country because of no visible means of support?" August asked Wolfgang as they headed back to the farm.

Then, all would be for naught. Rudolph would be back in Germany by fall and would surely be inducted into the army before spring.

"I need to declare an occupation for Rudolph and Adolph to make sure they are cleared for entry into the United States," August concluded.

A plan formed as the carriage traveled along. "I'll ask a favor of the village carpenter and another at the Rogasen grain mill. If the carpenter and miller agree, I'll have Rudolph work at the mill and Adolph with a carpenter, as apprentices without pay. These businessmen will agree — it will be good for them to have two hard workers for two weeks and for free. After a few weeks on the job, the boys should be convincing enough to satisfy the immigration inspectors. Also, they will each have an occupation to declare and ones that should be in demand in the United States."

August thought declaring as a farmer or farm laborer would be too easy to disallow entry for two young men without a definite farm address. Also, the Empire could decide farmers were too critical to its economy to allow leaving the country.

"Better to be safe," he said to Wolfgang as he trotted along toward Werdum. "A miller for Rudolph and a fancy work carpenter or joiner for Adolph," he mused. "That should work."

The boys were briefed by August after he had talked with both the carpenter and small gristmill owner. Each happily agreed to take them on — after all, they gained a free worker for two weeks or even more.

Though he felt somewhat relieved, August knew he wouldn't relax until he'd received a letter from the boys saying they'd passed inspection and were safely in New York City.

As August filled his sons in on the latest twist in the plan, he told them it probably felt like they were on a spinning wheel, but they'd better grab hold and hang on tight.

"This will be the adventure of a lifetime for you both," he told them.

CHAPTER FOUR

Departure

August's plan worked. The boys successfully completed their apprenticeships, working two weeks and more, right up to the last day before departure.

Rudolph and Adolph said their goodbyes to their friends the previous evening at the local beer garden in Werdum. It was a celebration to remember, especially for seventeen-year-old Adolph, who had very little prior exposure to the beer garden's happy times. Rudolph was now 20 years old, no longer a teenager, and he lorded his "maturity" over his younger sibling, much to Adolph's dislike. Nonetheless, all had a good time, especially the guests of honor. Their friends were of course sorry to see them leave but were somewhat envious as well. They let Wolfgang trot along at his own pace on the way home. They unhitched the carriage, tended to Wolfgang, stumbled upstairs, and tumbled into bed for a few hours' sleep.

Later that morning, as they loaded their trunks into the wagon, they realized this would probably be the last time they would see Werdum. The thought of being without family added to their sadness. They hugged and kissed each of their siblings and embraced their mother with heavy hearts, but their melancholy soon passed as August drove the carriage out of the farmyard onto the road to Rogasen and their adventure began.

Their railroad tickets, previously purchased by August during a Rogasen supply run, included connecting trains and covered travel from Rogasen to the large port city of Hamburg on the Elbe River. Once there, they would need to buy tickets to Bremen on the Weser River and then travel about 30 miles north, on a spur line, to the North Sea Port of Bremenhaven.

"Once there," August said, "go to the ship docks and look for a very large ship, the SS *Oder*. The ship agent in Posen told me it should be in port. If it isn't," he continued, "you'll have to rent a room on a daily basis until it arrives. It should arrive within a few days, depending on weather or engine problems."

They were early arriving at the train station, not wanting to miss their train to the seaport. The train had not yet arrived as Adolph tied Wolfgang to a hitching post and Rudolph pulled their two trunks off the carriage. The boys dragged them to the train platform and waited with their father.

August wanted to give them some worldly advice but found it difficult to do so. Rudolph and Adolph had expected some words of wisdom, and finally they came.

"Don't get involved with wayward women, don't spend money foolishly, and get a job in New York City."

After an hour or so wait, a train whistle was heard in the distance.

The boys said farewell to their father and picked out a passenger car, pulled their two trunks aboard, and placed them in the luggage rack in front of the car. Rosina had packed a lunch for their evening meal, and they took this with them to their seats.

Once on the train, they reviewed their travel plans. They would need to change trains at Stettin, transferring to a Hamburg-bound train arriving from Bromberg. They would need to buy tickets at Hamburg for a local train to Bremen and then continue to the North Sea, to the Port of Bremenhaven. There they would look for their ship, the SS *Oder*, which they hoped would already be at dockside.

The boys were transfixed for hours by the ever-changing scenery during their fascinating first-ever train ride. The Stettin transfer was made in early evening, after which the boys ate their evening lunch and then slept off and on as the steam locomotive wound its way through the dark German countryside. They arrived in Hamburg in the early morning and found their smaller train for the last leg of the journey to the town of Bremen and then on to Bremerhaven.

They arrived in Bremen very tired, but managed the transfer to the feeder line, a smaller train of only two cars. At last they arrived in Bremerhaven, nearly exhausted, both having found sleeping on the swaying and rocking rail cars very difficult.

They managed to rent a pull cart and trudged off to the docks some distance away from the train station, their trunks in tow on the cart. They were delighted to find the SS *Oder* had arrived two days previously. As promised, they were allowed to board even though departure was a few days away. They checked their trunks, took only essential personal gear, made sure their money belts were securely fastened, found their bunks, and collapsed into a light and somewhat apprehensive sleep.

The ship left port two days later. By this time, the boys were more comfortable and were making some friends in the surrounding bunk area. The SS *Oder's* route to the United States included a stop at Southhampton, England, to pick up more passengers. After this stop, there were 1,005 passengers on board, the vast majority in the lower priced steerage class.

At sea, their stomachs initially took a beating, but they were healthy young men, and after their stomachs settled, they traveled fairly well.

The food was basic but adequate. Hygiene went out the window, and privacy was practically nonexistent. Thus exposed to the rigors of ocean travel, Rudolph and Adolph began a journal to aid in writing their summary of ship travel. As instructed, they kept an accounting of significant daily events in steerage class, especially their stressful situations, and they used this diary to prepare a summary for their father.

They both lost weight due to a combination of meager food and lack of privacy, which added to their stress in subtle ways. The stench of a couple hundred people living in close quarters without adequate bathing facilities, ill infants, and seasick passengers all made for a very memorable journey, one they would never forget.

The ship arrived on schedule, taking two weeks for the crossing. The SS *Oder* navigated the New York Harbor straits between Staten and Manhattan Islands and anchored offshore for a disease check by a United States' Immigration Health Inspector. The Inspector looked at the ship's illness records and talked with the ship's doctor. Finding no reason to quarantine the vessel, disembarkation was started with smaller boats transporting groups of passengers to the immigration receiving station at the south end of Manhattan Island, Castle Gardens.

Rudolph and Adolph were happy to leave the immigration ship. They entered the large rotunda-shaped building called Castle Garden, apprehensive but excited. They observed the various inspection stations in the circular interior and prepared themselves for the expected questioning. They had purchased a German-to-English translation book at the big train station in Hamburg and had studied it during their ocean voyage, believing it would be very helpful during the questioning process. Even so, they were relieved to find some of the Castle Garden staff spoke German and were helpful to incoming immigrants.

The boys progressed through the various inspection stations without any real difficulty. They were both in good shape from their rigorous farm work, despite the recent shipboard weight loss. They were asked the key questions about occupation and work plans. The inspectors were inquisitive since the boys were traveling alone, but their short apprenticeships in Germany were of great value in describing their "documented work," as was their command of a few English words and phrases.

In turn, they received some tips and useful information from helpful staff members. Some of the staff were impressed that they had traveled on their own and would be staying two months or so in New York City, looking for jobs and awaiting their parents' arrival.

After successfully answering the inspectors' questions, being declared healthy, fit, and of right mind, and after exchanging money and finding their trunks, Rudolph and Adolph, along with many hundreds of fellow passengers, were released onto the streets of New York City on a sunny day in late May.

They had worked together to compose their letter during their last days aboard the SS *Oder* and had already mailed it at Castle Garden, so that task, too, was behind them.

Their parents were anxiously awaiting their report and were relieved when, in mid-June, they picked it up at the village post office.

August read their summary carefully and scanned the specific journal entries the boys included. They stated their specific entries would give them a more graphic picture of life in steerage. The steerage area was so named, they explained, because the location was below deck and close to the ship's steering mechanism. August grasped the details rapidly and then read it aloud to Rosina except for the steerage trivia.

The letter concluded, "We think our sisters and brothers can travel in steerage all right, but it will be hard. They won't be comfortable all the time and they can expect seasickness. But, maybe, if you get mild summer weather, they might even enjoy some of the trip."

Both August and Rosina studied the letter carefully. Although Rudolph had done the writing, both brothers had signed the letter to assure their father and mother they were of the same opinion.

August and Rosina had mixed emotions after reading the boy's trip summary and journal excerpts, but steerage class it was. Now for certain it was goodbye to Germany and their families. Sad to leave but happy at the thought of reuniting their family, August and Rosina immediately began finalizing their affairs and preparing for departure from Werdum.

The very next day, August hitched up Wolfgang and drove his buggy to Posen to arrange ship passage. He decided they could realistically tie up all their affairs in Werdum by early July.

The agent promised a ship assignment and date of departure in about a week. August then paid a deposit of 100 marks, with the balance due when he picked up the ticket receipt and travel information. It was dark when he drove into the farmyard, tired but happy in the knowledge that their journey would soon begin.

Upon returning to Posen a week later, he obtained firm information that a July passage was possible. They would depart from the Port of Hamburg, located in northern Germany on the Elbe River. Delighted, he completed payment of the passage fee, 561 marks in total, the equivalent of two or three years of profits. In return, he received a receipt for passage of two adults and five children leaving the Port of Hamburg on or about July 10, on the Hamburg American Line's steamer-sailor SS *Wieland*.

"Now," August said to Rose, "to deal with the farm owner regarding transfer of the farm to a new, suitable tenant." August and Rosina wanted the nobleman, who had been very good them over the years, to find a good tenant to take their place in running the farm especially with the farm animals in mind.

"Not so easy," said August, and he was right. The owner did not want them to leave but had no say in the matter, so he reluctantly agreed to look for another tenant.

August told the owner he would help look also, since he would like to find a suitable tenant to take over his beloved farm and animals, especially Wolfgang.

It was the least he could do, thought August. After all, he'd shared his innermost thoughts with Wolfgang.

"He was always understanding, and he never talked back," August chuckled out loud to Rosina.

August told the local beer garden owner his intentions and returned to the farm, knowing the news would spread. Two weeks passed without a move by the owner, although a number of candidates stepped forward. Finally, the nobleman selected a family August knew.

"Thank goodness," he told Wolfgang, "a good family will take over."

Both sets of parents hoped the move would fall through, but August's parents loaned money to the couple and August and Rosina purchased three large trunks for packing essential clothing and a few precious possessions, especially those that would remind them of their birthplace and life in Germany. These included the family Bible with historic events recorded in it, a small religious statue given as a wedding gift from Rosina's parents, a picture album, recent farm records of crop sales, names and addresses of friends, and some favorite clothes of Rosina's and the girls. The list of things they wanted to take to America was initially very large, but by necessity, was whittled down to fit the existing trunk space.

The items not taken were sold at an auction attended by the local farmers and interested village folks. Some people even came from Rogasen. Those items not sold were either given to the local church for distribution to the needy or transported to the village throwaway field.

August believed they had enough money to complete their travel to Michigan, with enough left, he thought, to carry them until he found work. This was a relief but they would be nearly starting from scratch again, since much of their savings would be used for travel. The little amount remaining, along with the loan money, would likely be needed to help them settle in the new country. August knew, if they were fortunate enough to rent a farm, extra money will be needed to outfit the farm, and maybe even to make the initial rent payment. August anticipated working hard to get a farm profitable and felt a responsibility to begin repaying his parent's loan on a yearly basis.

Prudently, he asked for and obtained a letter of introduction from the tenant farm owner attesting to his excellent payment record. That might be useful in Michigan, he decided.

Finally, with all loose ends tied up, the day of departure was upon them. August had exchanged the auction money and their savings for large denomination German currency. He put their savings, along with the family loan money, both in large denominations, into a money belt. He wrapped the belt around his girth and tied it securely under his shirt and coat.

Rosina's parents escorted them to the train station, having agreed to return their carriage to the farm in Werdum. It was August's last ride with Wolfgang, and he was sorry to say good-bye to his favorite horse and confidant.

He did so when they arrived at the train station, slipping him a bit of hardened sugar and a couple of nice carrots. Wolfgang munched happily as August patted his neck for the last time.

That sad task concluded, August spoke to his children.

"Now children," August said firmly, "you must always ask me for approval to take any side excursions. We need to stay together as much as possible — I don't want anyone to get lost. If I'm not available, you must always ask your mother for approval. This is very important."

August carefully took time to look each child in the eye and wait for a nod of acknowledgement. Temptations to wander were bound to occur, especially during a long journey with many train stops and a lengthy ship voyage.

August's parents were also on hand, and together on the loading platform, the family said their tearful goodbyes and boarded the train while August remained on the platform to observe their three large trunks being loaded. When this was complete, he boarded and found his family snugly seated with their three carrying bags, looking forward to an entertaining train ride to Stettin, then on to Hamburg and the North Sea

The train engine's drive wheels spun on the steel tracks as the train operator impatiently gave it more steam to accelerate out of the small town of Rogasen.

"We're on the way to the North Sea!" Adolphine said excitedly. The entire family was very excited, as well they should be, except for four-year-old Bertha, who was fast asleep nestled against her mother.

They arrived without incident at the train station in the port city of Hamburg having transferred, like Rudolph and Adolph, in the town of Stettin, about 110 miles to the northwest of Rogasen. They had previously decided the children could sleep on the train, which would allow them to travel the next 190 miles overnight to Hamburg.

None of the family had traveled by train before, so the children, as well as their parents, were highly entertained by the passing landscape and by observing the new passengers as they boarded at subsequent stops.

Rosina had brought farm cheese, homemade bread, and sausage along with a large jug of fresh well water for traveling.

This also helped keep the children content. The coal-fired steam engine moved the train steadily through the German countryside, and August was reminded of the mineral wealth in the previously held French states of Lorraine and Alsace.

"The Alsace-Lorraine region," he said, "was one of the factors in our decision to leave." He looked at Frederick and Emiel, both sleeping by this time, and was convinced the dramatic migration decision, with its ensuing life changes, was the right thing to do.

August had timed their Hamburg arrival two days before their scheduled departure and had been assured by the Posen ticket office that if the ship were already in port, they could board upon arrival. He reasoned this would help keep travel complexity to a minimum since overnight lodging at Stettin or Hamburg would not be necessary.

Before leaving the train, the family double-checked the seat area to ensure their carry-on bags and other travel items were in tow. August and the young boys pulled their three trunks from the storage rack in front of the rail car and arranged for a wagon to transport them from the train station to dockside. They arrived dockside to happily find the SS *Wieland* already in port.

August and Rosina's biggest fear was losing one of their five children, ages 4 to 14, during their long journey. Reducing complexity was important to them, since they anticipated enough confusion during the journey. Traveling for nearly 24 hours straight on the train had been physically challenging, and getting settled immediately on board the ship, in their tired state, was going to be stressful. But both August and Rosina believed it would minimize the chances of someone getting lost and greatly reduce the complexity of overnight lodgings with five children.

As a precaution, they also used a tag system, assigning each of the younger boys to an older sibling, except for energetic Bertha. She would be under Rosina's constant careful watch. In addition, they required each of the children to keep a small piece of paper with the Woltman's Michigan address pinned to their underclothing at all times.

The tired Mallast family boarded the ship with anxious anticipation that morning in July of 1882. Rosina clutched Bertha's hand tightly and warned the other four children to stay together. Such was the start of the family's ocean travel to a new continent.

They checked their trunks onboard as required before proceeding to their assigned family bunk area, and then they settled into their assigned meager bunk space.

"Thank goodness our sons bravely went before us," August said to Rosina, "warning us in advance about these cramped and gloomy conditions. It's less of a surprise this way."

As August looked lovingly at his young family, he worried about their welfare these next weeks and months. "I pray the weather will be good during the crossing," he said out loud. "This is home for two weeks or more depending on weather and equipment breakdowns," he reminded them.

Soon, the migration to North America was underway. The ship left the dock at Hamburg on a stormy July morning, steaming out into the harbor with the single stack billowing large clouds of black smoke. The immigration vessel moved slowly past anchored ships waiting for dock space and some smaller boats transporting people from dock to ships and vise versa. The SS *Wieland* was sailing for the United States, carrying hundreds of Central Europeans, all hoping for a better life in North America.

August felt relief that their children could grow, mature, and live their lives in a country with only two neighboring nations. Germany's proximity to its many neighbors with conflicting agendas could, and often did, result in sour relations that sometimes turned into wars.

August felt happy to have the full support and agreement of his wife, and he eagerly anticipated finding out if the glowing picture the Woltman family had painted of life in America was realistic. In addition to abundant farmland with fresh water and magnificent agricultural soil, the cost of land, per the Woltmans, was much lower than equivalent properties in Germany.

"The lower land prices may be an exaggeration; I'll believe it when I see it," he privately told Rosina. "Even if there are lower prices, I anticipate not being able to buy a farm, especially since most of our savings are being used for the voyage and travel in America. Hopefully, we will be able to rent." Even though he didn't expect to be able to buy land, he felt good about the decision to leave and their prospects in their new country.

The SS *Wieland* used only steam power as it navigated the channel and steamed up the harbor. It moved steadily out of the harbor, turning northwest into the turbulent North Sea. Sails were hoisted after clearing the harbor, and the work of tacking the ship southwest and northwest began. Slowly, the ship moved westward down the English Channel, despite the steady western wind.

August found he had mixed emotions as he stood on the crowded deck with many other families and watched their homeland slip into the distance and finally disappear from sight.

For many, like the Mallasts, it had been tough to leave their established way of life in Germany and other Central

European countries. For others, the decision to leave was easy. But for almost all the travelers, expectations were high. Some anticipated acquiring more land than they could possibly own in Europe. They looked forward to rich agricultural soil and abundant fresh water. Some western land was rumored to be free for the taking, just for homesteading, which involved preparing the land for farming. This would mean cutting trees and clearing brush from fields. This was hard work, but the reward was unheard of in Europe. Also, reportedly, land was available at much lower prices than in Germany. Furthermore, some realized, as did August, that no major political conflicts loomed on the horizon in North America.

The established course was westerly, into the English Channel with a stop at Le Havre, France, to pick up more passengers. The vessel was a 375-foot steamer-sailor with two masts for sails and one belching smoke stack. The steam engine was tucked in the rear of the 40-foot wide, long steel hull. The engine powered a screw propeller, which moved the ship at about 13 knots per hour in calm seas but much slower in rough seas, frequently encountered with the strong prevailing westerly winds. The twin powers of sail and steam gave the captain and the crew a confident, relaxed feeling should the wind not cooperate or mechanical failures occur with the relatively new technology of the coal-fired, steam-powered engine.

The ship was designed to accommodate 190 passengers in first- and second-class cabins and approximately 800 in steerage. After taking on passengers at Le Havre, the steerage head count was 861 and the first- and second-class number at 122. Nearly a thousand souls were aboard the ship, at the mercy of mother nature and the seaworthiness of the SS *Wieland*.

August could not help but think of the stories of lost ships at sea but kept such thoughts to himself. "No need to alarm Rosina," he said to himself. With quarters so tight, shipboard friends were made easily. So many migrating families aboard, sharing similar excitement and concerns, created an environment conducive to conversation, especially for the outgoing Rosina and her twin girls.

August, more reserved and thoughtful, concentrated on carefully determining each major phase of travel before actually getting into each situation. He worried about possible problems and went over contingency plans for each of his perceived challenges. He found his long skinny pipe a great comfort and was grateful he had taken care to ensure he had enough tobacco in his small, accessible personal bag to keep his thinking companion well stoked during the journey across the Atlantic Ocean.

The children were excited prior to the journey; however, their excitement subsided soon after departure and remained so until their systems were well purged and their landlubber stomachs adjusted.

Food, by law, was provided on board the immigration ships. It was basic fare, usually including potatoes, bread, bacon or smoked sausage or dried fish. Breakfast was typically ground grains and a biscuit with coffee and water. The midday meal included a thin soup, either bread or a biscuit, hard cheese, and sausage. The evening meal consisted of baked potatoes and salted pork, with the occasional dried fish or boiled sausage.

Of course, good German beer was a favorite beverage. It was also a necessary "medicine" for those who wanted to avoid scurvy. This illness, caused by a lack of vitamin C, was a real concern during the two-plus weeks' passage to North America.

Captains used this convincing argument to ensure a more than adequate beer supply before departure.

Beer was also a source of clean drinking liquid during the journey, since it was difficult to store drinking water aboard the vessels for long periods. It took on unsavory characteristics, requiring rum and lemon juice to make it a palatable drink — called grog.

The children did not look forward to their nightly glass of required anti-scurvy "medicine." They did not yet like the bitter taste of the brew but even so, the eight- and eleven-year-old boys, mimicking their father, pretended to like the golden liquid "medicine." They found the ship's food to be adequate although not nearly as delicious as their mother's meals on the farm. The exception was eight-year-old Fred, who very much enjoyed eating and found even the ship's fare to be tasty.

Bertha's system got used to the change in diet but only after the rough seas took their toll. Rosina tried to mitigate Bertha's nausea by keeping her meals very basic, but there wasn't much she could do, since the meals themselves were very basic. Almost all the migrating passengers had stomach adjustments to make.

Quarters were tight, to say the least. Bunk beds ran in rows down the length of the steerage class three beds high, with each bunk sleeping two people. The three-high bunk beds had been in use for some years, the vessel being about eight years old when outfitted for immigration transport.

Families were kept together. There were no bathing facilities, but there were washbasins for sea water. Each day, sea water was pumped up for daily deck washing and the crew accommodated those passengers wishing a hose wash down over light clothing. The smell of hundreds of people traveling in tight quarters, especially during rough weather, when no passengers were allowed on deck, was memorable and sometimes nearly unbearable. This, coupled with wet diaper odors and nausea during storm periods, added to the foul fragrance, just as Rudolph and Adolph had warned.

Many people in steerage had come from meager means and were not healthy; they suffered more than the farm-bred Mallasts. Some passengers did perish during the crossing and were mourned by their transient friends.

By the time the SS *Wieland* left France in its wake, most of the Hamburg passengers had adjusted to the roll of the English Channel, but now they encountered the real challenge for their stomachs: the heavy North Atlantic swells. The ship moved straight into the teeth of the ever blowing, prevailing strong westerly winds, tacking constantly to make forward progress toward America. Although it was nearly 375 feet long, the vessel's sides were exposed to the heavy rollers as it tacked southward and then northward repeatedly, and the constant up and down rocking and rolling in the heavy troughs played havoc with their stomachs.

Upon leaving Hamburg and Le Havre, the passengers were systematically assembled into small groups of one representative from each family. Then, one group at a time, they were briefed on survival by the ship's officers. They were told how the lifeboats would be deployed and instructed on life belt usage. The cork life belts were on deck in a central storage area with the passengers to grab one as they filed past while officers would take responsibility for loading each lifeboat.

August, having been in large groups in the army, could only imagine the chaos that would ensue if there were an emergency.

He remembered reading an account of a ship that had sunk a few years earlier, the SS *Geiser*. The captain reported that the 700 life belts, easily accessible to all, were virtually unused in the panic, in spite of the crews' urging to the contrary. Also, one of the eight lifeboats had sunk, having been incorrectly launched, its stern plunging into the sea in a near vertical attitude and sinking immediately.

August counted eight lifeboats on the SS *Wieland* and wondered if they could contain all the passengers.

When he saw the Atlantic's large 10- to 12-foot rollers, he realized prospects for survival would be very slim for the mass of humanity on board the vessel if it were to sink. He prayed hard for a safe passage.

After a few days, the ocean calmed a bit and they adjusted nicely to the ship's constant but moderate rocking and rolling. The wind decreased somewhat, although it still blew stiffly and steadily from the west. Accordingly, the rollers too subsided somewhat, and they all breathed a sigh of relief.

During the voyage, fourteen-year-old Emielie developed her first crush, on a handsome young teenage crewman. She was smitten by a young eighteen-year-old crewmember, Eric. She would stroll the deck in calm weather, making short excursions up and down the deck, discretely looking for Eric. He soon got the message, as teenagers tend to do. Conversations were brief during his work periods but a meeting place was established near the front mast where, as Emielie told her mother, they would meet and just talk. Rosina was more astute than her daughter gave her credit for and did occasionally stroll the deck herself during Emielie's absence, tactfully undetected but observant.

Emielie and Eric got along well. They talked of his life in Germany before signing aboard his first ship, the SS *Wieland*. After a few meetings, they managed their first kiss, being careful Rosina was not in sight. Emielie urged Eric to leave the ship and live with the Mallasts in their new homeland. Eric, half sincere, promised he would think about it. He gave Emielie his mailing address in Germany since he realized the probability of migrating to America was very, very remote.

Rosina knew the hormones were flowing in Emielie and probably Eric as well, and she confided in August. "Emielie wants Eric to move with us to Michigan."

Wisely, August told Rosina not to be too concerned. "Let it play out," he said. "We'll be off the ship in a few weeks but we need to be astute and keep the curfew in effect. You might also have another mother-daughter talk with her."

When the two weeks had passed, Emielie was happy to leave the ship although heartsick to leave Eric. They had a last evening under the front mast, kissing passionately until Emielie's nine o'clock curfew time arrived. She said goodbye tearfully, knowing she would not see Eric again except in leaving the ship the next morning.

It was a lasting experience for Emielie — her first but not last crush.

This added to Rosina's anxiety, since Emielie's interests and those of eleven-year-old Emiel were in different directions. Emiel was fascinated by the mechanics of the steam engine and the art of sailing. Exasperated, Rosina wondered if Adolphine, too, would also be smitten during the coming weeks.

"That would be impossible to manage," she confided to August.

The SS *Wieland*, having adequate freeboard and being heavily ballasted, rode the large waves more easily than the passengers, and the ship arrived at New York Harbor intact in two weeks time, just as anticipated.

The ship's crew did not encounter a major problem, although steam power gave out once. The sails were much appreciated at that time, being independent of mechanical part failures. They sailed steadily on, moving always in a general westerly direction by executing long tacks into the ever blowing, stiff westerly wind.

The mechanical problem was immediately apparent, with steam issuing from a failed gasket in the high pressure feed line to the power cylinder. It was repaired after boiler cool down with installation of a replacement gasket. Steam power restored, their pace quickened as sailing power was augmented by the rotating propeller.

It was an adventure they would always remember, especially Emielie.

CHAPTER FIVE

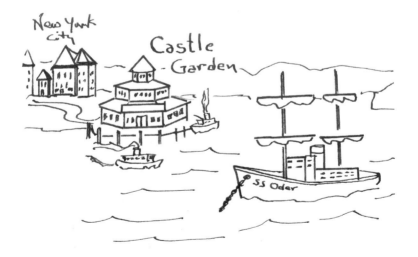

Arrival in America and Life in New York City

The sun was shining as Rudolph and Adolph prepared to step outside Castle Garden. Each had brought a travel trunk from Werdum, but they'd been required to check them before boarding the SS *Oder* in Bremerhaven. They were told to keep their claim tags if they wanted to reclaim them in America.

They were apprehensive while the Castle Garden staff tried to find their trunks in the mass of luggage unloaded from the SS *Oder*. These contained their only possessions in the new world and their only connection with their former home in Prussia, so they each breathed a sigh of relief when they saw them emerge, one by one, from the large stack of luggage at the Castle Garden's exit point.

Their next challenge was to face the expected onslaught of runners, otherwise known as hustlers, immediately outside the gate. Mr. Woltman had described his family's experience, so Rudolph and Adolph were braced for this next hurdle.

Sometimes a runner would sell something on promise, only to skip out and not deliver the item purchased or the personal service promised. Thus, the boys were wary. Although tired, they refused offers to have their trunks delivered ahead of them to a "good, reasonable boarding house." They were not going to let those trunks out of their possession, and after all, they were their only link to their boyhood home in Prussia.

They also refused offers to transport them and their trunks, especially since they didn't know what a reasonable fee would be. They didn't want to be charged too much, and they also considered the possibility of being waylaid by pre-positioned partners of an unscrupulous driver with the upshot being stolen trunks.

As they made their way through the throng of hustlers, they kept their trunks' draw ropes tightly in their hands. Unlike Bremerhaven, there were no pull carts to rent, and the trunks were not extremely large or heavy so they decided to drag them to the recommended boarding house. The few changes of clothes and a few necessities for single young men did not weigh a great deal so they were able to pull them without a great deal of effort.

A kindly German-speaking staff member had given them a Castle Garden street map dispensed to emerging immigrants. He had also recommended a boarding house and written the name next to a large handwritten "X" marking its location. Thoughtfully, he had also included some relatively easy-to-spot landmarks to aid in their street navigation.

Map in hand, Rudolph and Adolph set out to find the boarding house, navigating the streets of New York City with only a few errors, most of the time heading in the general direction toward the large "X" on their New York City map.

They were in awe of the large city and the commotion and hustle of people, horse carriages, and wagons on the crowded streets as they walked from the southern tip of Manhattan Island toward New York's city center. They were so thankful for the map. After about two hours of dragging their trunks, with stops to rest every 20 minutes or so, they sighted the boarding house. Again Rudolph grasped the English-German translation book as they entered the building on Canal Street, trunks in tow. It was nearly a two-mile distance from the southern tip of the island and they were tired.

They found the owner and, using their translation book, asked if a room was available. They told the owner their parents would migrate from Prussia later that year and that they would like to stay at his boarding house until they arrived, assuming they could afford the cost.

A room was available and the price in line with the information given by the Castle Garden staff member.

Immediately upon settling in, the boys wrote to their parents again, giving the name and address of their newfound home.

As helpful as their translation book was at Castle Garden and the boarding house, it was even more so in handling their bustling new surroundings, so foreign from their previous and rather isolated life on the farm. This was a very different and very exciting time for the boys, but they were up for the challenge.

They had exchanged their German marks for United States dollars, so they proudly paid the landlord's required first week's room and board with United States dollars. They had enough money to carry them until the family arrived, but nonetheless, they were expected to look for jobs to help pay their way during this time.

August had explained the family needed to save every mark they could during the journey to support them until they found jobs or were able to rent or buy a farm in Michigan.

"Also," he had told his sons, "you will be much better occupied with jobs than just twiddling your thumbs waiting for the family to arrive. You would have too much idle time and be bored out of your minds."

August had also thought to himself that jobs should keep them occupied and hopefully keep them out of trouble. Too much idle time might lead to some mischief during their time alone in a big city.

Accordingly, the boys had asked about job possibilities at the Castle Garden Labor Exchange Station and were given a few leads, but dozens of other immigrants were also seeking employment in New York City.

The boys also asked their landlord and their newfound boarding house "quasi-family" about the possibility of jobs. Many suggestions followed, which they pursued aggressively. They did a lot of walking all over the city, and it paid off when Rudolph, age 20, found a helper's job at one of the numerous saloons in the large city. But a job was offered to Rudolph only, since Adolph was only 17.

Rudolph was at home in the saloon surroundings, and this would serve him well at a later date. He was likeable, he didn't hesitate to talk to patrons with his limited English, interspersed with German words and phrases, and he used a lot of hand gestures as he kept tables tidy or helped serve drinks for the waiters. His broken English instilled amused interest and continued conversations with interested and curious customers. He inquired of co-workers and some friendly-looking patrons about work for his younger brother, pursuing each suggestion with Adolph during his off hours.

In about a week, Adolph, too, landed a job. It was at a large lunchroom, serving the numerous office workers in the city. But transportation was a problem since it was a long, long walk from their boarding house. Adolph and Rudolph checked out the public horse-drawn streetcars and found they could reach the lunchroom in about a half hour, with only one transfer.

All told, the boys did well and were both employed and occupied while they waited for the family to arrive sometime in the summer or early fall.

Family Arrives

As the end of July neared, the SS *Wieland* had the continent in sight. The ship was relatively on course and only a slight correction in heading was needed. The captain ordered the sails lowered and the ship steamed slowly through the New York straits and anchored in sight of a busy dockside scene.

Crewmembers were asked repeatedly for information about the new land, and they generally passed on information as time and dispositions allowed.

Most had been working for a number of years on the Germany-to-America run and by now knew just about every question that could be asked.

Information was also shared among some of the passengers who, like the Mallasts, had received letters from families or friends who had preceded them in their migration to North America. The families were anxious as they anticipated transitioning from seafaring travelers to processing immigrant status.

As with the boys' ship, an Immigration Health Inspector boarded to determine if there was an epidemic or widespread illnesses among the passengers. If any were detected, the ship would be placed in quarantine at a harbor island and the passengers would not be allowed on the mainland until the epidemic was checked and the passengers declared healthy. Ill passengers would be placed in a quarantine hospital on Staten Island in New York Harbor.

After checking the SS *Wieland's* ship's log and talking with the ship's doctor and the ship's captain, the inspector declared the ship epidemic-free and allowed the crew to begin disembarking the passengers.

The immigrants were organized into groups and loaded into smaller vessels and barges for transportation by water to the Castle Garden receiving station. The luggage was transported in mass to Castle Garden, there to be stacked in a large area near the exiting doors. They were told the luggage would be released on a family-by-family basis, after the immigration checks were successful completed. Once luggage was in hand, the new arrivals would be allowed to step out onto the streets of New York.

Eric was on deck that morning, helping to unload the mountain of luggage. His coworkers were sympathetic to his plight and allowed him some spare time to say a sad farewell to Emielie. Such was the end of their short teenage love affair.

The Mallasts, as well as the others, were very happy to leave their home at sea. All, that is, except for boy-struck Emielie. Although Emielie's romance had ended, the family's adventures in the United States were only beginning.

The family stuck together on deck, waiting their turn, and after about an hour, they were aboard one of the boats bound for Castle Garden.

The building, positioned on a rock island just off the southern end of Manhattan Island, had been constructed in the early 1800s as an entertainment facility for New York City.

It was converted to an immigrant receiving station as the need became apparent during the mid-1800s.

Their sons' description of the immigration process was very helpful in allaying August's and Rosina's apprehensions and preparing them for some of the key questions the inspectors would ask them. A number of different inspection stations, each looking for a specific health problem, awaited them. If discovered, the prospective immigrant could be denied entrance into the United States or moved to the quarantine facility in the bay on Statin Island, devoted solely to that purpose.

The Mallasts were all reasonably healthy, having avoided the illnesses carried by some of the passengers during the journey, and the questioning went well. August had come prepared with some English words and phrases, but most of the time German-speaking staff members, on duty specifically to translate, assisted. They progressed through the various inspection stations.

Those immigrants deemed acceptable were released in waves or small groups, first finding and verifying ownership of their trunks and luggage stacked near the Castle Garden street exit. Castle Garden staff was on hand to facilitate this process and to check the trunk and luggage ownership claim tags against the actual luggage tags.

With the families' successful completion of the immigration process and retrieval of their trunks, they were now ready to step out onto the streets of one of the largest cities in their new land. With their luggage in tow, the Mallasts, along with hundreds of other families and individuals, were ushered out of the station and expelled onto the streets of New York City, dragging all their worldly possessions with them.

August and Rosina dragged one trunk each, with carrying bags held by Emielie and Adolphine. Bertha stayed close to Rosina and had no trouble keeping up. The young boys, Emiel and Fred, each grabbed a pull rope on the third trunk and were able to keep up as well. They all hoped to see Rudolph and Adolph, but they were not in sight.

August had written to Rudolph and Adolph before leaving Prussia, immediately after learning the ship's name and departure date. He wanted the letter to reach them with plenty of time so they could meet their ship upon arrival. Consequently, he and Rosina were surprised and disappointed their sons were not on hand to greet them. Rosina in particular had built herself up for a very happy reunion the minute they left Castle Garden.

Though disappointed, the busy streets and enthusiastic attempts by runners to sell their wares and services kept the family in awe. Meanwhile, the thoughtful August launched into his backup plan.

Clutching the boys' handwritten directions to their boarding house in his hand, he guided the family from Castle Garden to a wagon stop and gave the map to the driver after agreeing on a fee. The boys had included some information about wagon fees in their letter, so he handled the price hassling quite well.

They hoisted the trunks onto the wagon bed and the driver let the children ride up front on the wagon. August and Rosina walked briskly alongside, buoyed by their tremendous accomplishment, excited to see the boarding house, and wondering what had become of their sons.

Rudolph had indeed received his father's letter with ship sailing information about a week prior to the expected arrival date. He had scanned the boarding house newspaper every night, looking for notice of the SS *Wieland's* landing. He'd finally spotted the ship's arrival date and had arranged to have that afternoon off so he could greet his parents and siblings at Castle Garden, but he hoped they'd taken the boarding house address with them in case he couldn't find them in the crowd.

Adolph, meanwhile, intended to go straight to the boarding house immediately after his lunchroom job was over, as excited as Rudolph to see the family again.

Rudolph went to the Castle Garden exit area as planned, but with the exiting hundreds of immigrants, some friends and relatives, and the runners, he was not able to spot his parents. The crowd was too large. After fruitlessly searching for his family for some time, he returned to the boarding house. There he found his family anxiously waiting.

What a happy reunion on that street in New York City!

Rudolph explained that Adolph would join them after work, and he proudly escorted them into the boarding house and up to the room he had arranged for them.

August had exchanged his German marks for United States currency at the Castle Garden Exchange Brokers. Concerned about protecting their money as they traveled to Michigan, he'd kept his new United States bills clutched tightly inside his coat pocket on their travel to the boarding house. Once inside their room at the boarding house, he'd transferred the bills to a money belt, tied the belt pockets tightly with double knots, and then tied the belt tightly around his girth.

That night, he'd slept uneasily with it under his pillow. The door had been locked, but two windows stood wide open. Their room was above street level, so August thought it was safe to sleep with open windows, but it still worried him. Nonetheless, it was necessary, as the current mid-summer weather was very hot, especially in the city.

A day of rest followed, with time for a thorough bath for each from head to toe, some tasty food at the boarding house, and a grand lunch next day at Adolph's workplace.

August, of course, with Adolph as his nighttime guide, had to check out Rudolph's workplace. Adolph guided well, and they enjoyed celebrating Rudolph's last night at the popular east side saloon.

The boys' employers knew these hard-working, energetic young men would be leaving New York City, and they were sorry to see them go. Accordingly, both were extended grateful goodbyes by their respective employers. Thus Rudolph's and Adolph's two-month stay in New York City flew by and came to a close all too fast to suit the brothers.

The next morning, after breakfast at the boarding house, August removed some bills from his money belt. This morning he removed $40.00, a sizeable amount, based on Rudolph's advice. Rudolph had engaged in conversations at the saloon and was advised that $40.00 should be enough to buy nine train tickets to Michigan. August, not wanting to remove his shirt in public, carried the money in his pocket.

August and Rudolph set out for the train station to purchase tickets for travel to Michigan. They were given directions at the boarding house, with a suggestion to take a streetcar because it was a long walk. August, unsure about using an unknown form of transportation, told Rudolph the walk would be good for him.

So off they set, leaving their boarding house on Canal Street and headed up Broadway toward the Grand Central Depot. They were told Grand Central Depot was located on 42nd Street near

Madison Avenue and quite a walk from their boarding house. But August countered that it gave him another chance to see New York City. Well into the walk, Rudolph bravely chided his father about the long walk but August said, "You must be getting soft! Exercise is good for you!"

An hour later, having completed the hike of two and a half miles, they reached Grand Central Depot on Madison Avenue and entered the "Hudson" tower.

August did not purchase train tickets at the Castle Garden Railway Agency, since he did not know the boys' situations with their employers. "Enough of this traveling separately," he told Rosina. "I'm not about to have the family separated on the last leg of our journey to Michigan."

A ticket agent at the New York Central and Hudson River line, located in the left tower of the Grand Central Depot, gave August ticket and travel information. This was all way beyond August's understanding, but Rudolph now understood enough English to grasp the jest of the transfer information and they purchased tickets for train travel from New York City to Toledo, Ohio, and transfer tickets to Detroit, Michigan.

Rudolph understood a New York Central and Hudson Railroad train departed every morning, traveling north, up the Hudson River to Albany. There, they would transfer to a west-bound train to Buffalo, New York. The agent recommended they stay overnight in Buffalo and, with August's concurrence, Rudolph confirmed they would. The tickets were issued accordingly and the agent explained they would need to travel on a different railroad, the Lake Shore and Michigan Southern, after the overnight stay in Buffalo.

The agent saw the confused look on Rudolph's face and explained, "But don't worry, it's a different line but it is owned by New York Central, so your tickets are good even though it's a different name. Your train is bound for Chicago. There are three stops along the way; Cleveland, Toledo, and South Bend."

The agent told Rudolph they needed to get off at Toledo and then proceed north to Detroit. He cautioned Rudolph not to leave at the first stop, but stay on the train until it reached Toledo, the second stop.

They would need to transfer to a feeder line that ran from Toledo to Detroit while the main line train proceeded to Chicago.

"You're in luck," the agent told Rudolph. "We leased a railroad line that runs from Toledo to Detroit about 10 years ago. So you will stay with the Lake Shore and Michigan Southern Railroad, which means your luggage will be transferred for you all the way to Detroit. The line we leased was called the 'Detroit, Monroe and Toledo Railroad'" the agent continued. "Good to remember in case the Toledo crew still refers to the Detroit connection by the old name."

"The Grand Trunk Train Company has a lake line that runs north from Detroit, about 60 miles to the southern tip of Lake Huron. Along the way, it has several stops, one of which is Mt. Clemens."

The agent's use of city names was foreign to August and Rudolph except for Mt. Clemens. He explained, "Your large trunks will be checked in on this platform for travel up the Hudson River to Albany. There, the trunks will be off-loaded but retained at the terminal for your train to Toledo, and then transferred to the train for Detroit. In Detroit, you will need to buy tickets for a local line, the Grand Trunk Railroad, going to Port Huron with stops along the way, including Mt. Clemens. You will need to claim your trunks in Detroit, probably arriving before you do, and carry them to the Grand Trunk Railroad. You might have to hire a wagon to get them there. I'm not sure, but the Grand Trunk Station might be at a different location than the station we use in Detroit. Not sure but at least you're forewarned."

Rudolph thanked him for the explanation. August, not understanding most of the conversation, hoped Rudolph did and got ready to pay for the tickets.

"Did you follow all that, Rudolph?" said August.

"Not really but I got the gist of it, although we may need to ask questions along the way. I found most people here are anxious to help with directions," replied Rudolph.

The money August brought with him was sufficient to pay for the tickets to Detroit. The total cost was $17.20. Each adult ticket cost $2.70, the children's tickets cost $1.35, and little Bertha's ticket was $1.00.

August tucked the tickets and remaining money in his pocket and they returned to the boarding house. He kept his hand in his pocket the entire way to protect the tickets and his money.

The sun had been beating down on the city all morning and continued to do so as August and Rudolph began their hike back to the boarding house. As they walked briskly along the hot streets they were sweating profusely, nearly soaked at the end of the hour jaunt. Rosina took one look and ordered them immediately to the bath tub down the hall.

Rosina was delighted to learn they were leaving the following morning. She feared one or more of the five youngsters would wander from the boarding house if they stayed much longer.

August, now aware of the distance from the boarding house to the train station, let Rudolph arrange for a horse and wagon to transport their trunks and hand luggage from the boarding house to the train station. Arriving at the station early next morning, they checked their trunks at the Hudson Line terminal and joined many other traveling families awaiting train passage inland. They were pleased to see some of the locals selling basic foodstuffs including bread, cheese, sausage, and fresh milk.

The fresh milk at the boarding house was a welcome sight for the family, especially for Rosina, since it hadn't been available on the ship. Bertha drank two glasses at their supper and another two the following morning at breakfast.

They boarded the train to Albany, then transferred to a westward bound train to Buffalo. Following an evening at a Buffalo hotel, they continued westward to Toledo, handling the 800 miles of train travel and transfers quite well. After all, they now had some experience, all of two days of European train travel under their belts.

All the children were accounted for so far, but the curious young teenage boys, Emiel and Fitz (their nickname for Fred) were prone to wander, which kept Rosina and August on their toes and tempers a little on edge.

And the older teenage twin girls weren't too far behind, always exploring for handsome boys to talk with, or any boys to talk with.

Food was taken aboard each leg of the passage and overnight stay was arranged in Toledo. The family was excited, anticipating completion of the travel to Mt. Clemens on the following day. Their long journey would be over, and they would see their correspondence friends, the Woltmans, for the first time.

Boarding houses, furnishing accommodations to travelers, had sprung up at or near the large cities' train stations. These establishments were accustomed to serving immigrants traveling west, so August found that securing lodgings was easier than expected.

Their long journey of nearly a month, preceded by many months of planning, was nearing an end. But Rudolph was a bit apprehensive, expecting difficulty in the transfer in Detroit, having remembered the New York agent saying something about renting a horse and wagon. He didn't understand it all, he told his father.

"Too much information in such a short time. I need to find an agent to ask what we do in Detroit to find the next train line we need to get to Mt. Clemens. Don't leave without me," he added jokingly as he walked away.

Rudolph waited in line to talk to a ticket agent. Finally up to the window, Rudolph showed the agent his ticket and asked, "We are going to Mt. Clemens, Michigan, beyond Detroit. What do we do once we get to Detroit?"

The agent had heard the transfer "What do we do?" question many times and was well prepared with an answer.

"I see you're traveling to Detroit on the old Detroit, Monroe and Toledo line. You're in luck, since this line terminates at the Brush Street Station, which is owned by the train line you need to take to Mt. Clemens, the Grand Trunk. This means you won't have to leave the station and rent a horse and wagon to transport your trunks to another location. That would be the case if you were taking another line, such as Michigan Central. The Detroit station you'll be going to is called the Brush Street Station, while, for example, the Michigan Central line uses a different one, called the 3rd Street Station. More than you wanted to know but hope you understand. Once in Detroit, you need to claim your trunks and connect with a different train line, the Grand Trunk Railroad. You need to transfer to the Grand Trunk Railroad to get to Mt. Clemens. Then buy a ticket and find the departure platform. It's pretty straightforward," concluded the ticket agent as he returned Rudolph's ticket.

Rudolph was relieved and told August the good news. "It won't be nearly as complicated as I feared," he said.

Once in Michigan, August felt a great sense of relief. They'd left Germany with three large trunks and three hand-carried luggage bags. Now, standing in the Detroit train station, they had only two large trunks. The boys had their smaller trunks and their hand-carried bags were all accounted for but someone had missed transferring one of the three large trunks.

"It must have been at one of the three New York Central transfer points; Albany, Buffalo, or Toledo," said August. "I'll tell the ticket agent we're missing a trunk!"

The Detroit agent sent a telegraph message to the New York Central office in Toledo, reporting the missing trunk. The agent had some experience with missing trunks and said he expected a reply in a few days. He asked them to check with the Grand Trunk agent in Mt. Clemens in a few days. "We might have some information at that time," he told August.

Getting their missing trunk could take a week or more per the train agent in Detroit, but this minor problem did not dampen the Mallasts' excited moods as they boarded the Grand Trunk train headed north to Port Huron, with a stop at their final destination, Mount Clemens.

The train pulled out of the Detroit station with the Mallasts safely aboard, albeit without all of their luggage. They started the last leg of train travel in an apprehensive but excited mood. They were told it was 20 miles to Mt. Clemens and it would take about two hours with stops along the way. During their train ride north, their excitement and curiosity grew with every stop.

A fellow traveler sensed their situation from their excited talk and inquisitive body language. He introduced himself and described the region as the steam engine chugged its way north from Detroit. His parents had migrated from Germany when he was a pre-teen but he could still speak German, enough for the Mallasts to understand. He told them Mt. Clemens was initially settled by the French but German immigrants had moved into the area, perhaps led by mercenaries who had fought on either side during the American Revolution or the war of 1812.

Regardless, during the 1800s, a number of German families had put down stakes in this Midwestern part of the United States. Their hard work ethic and farming skills were put to an easy test in mostly fertile land, in the water-abundant Michigan.

Of course, they had been unable to get word to the Woltmans of their exact arrival day. August had written them of their general plan in late June, so the Woltmans should expect them to arrive in late summer. August had reasoned that a letter written in July, mailed in Germany, would probably not move much faster than their travel speed. Sometimes, he reasoned, it could move slower due to missed or inefficient ship or train connections. Surprises were sometimes fun to experience, thought August as he completed his rationalization.

Thus, the Mallasts found themselves standing on the Mount Clemens train station platform, two of their three trunks in tow, on that late afternoon in August. August felt his money belt and was reassured — so far so good.

He hired a driver with horse and wagon to transport them to the Sherman House hotel, as suggested by the Woltmans. It was centrally located on Court Street, the main street through town. Next morning, getting directions at the desk, he and Rudolph set out walking to find the Woltmans. Adolph would stay with Rosina to help manage his younger siblings.

For her part, Mrs. Woltman was not too surprised when August and Rudolph appeared out of the blue at their house in Mount Clemens. She greeted them warmly and invited them back that evening when her husband would be home from work.

The Mallasts arrived shortly after dinner and again were greeted warmly. They discussed the local terrain, general living conditions, and job situation at great length. Heinrich gave the Mallasts some background on the area as well. "A Christian Clemens surveyed the land about 1800 and mapped out the town. As you might tell from looking down on the river, the town is on a rise, but the surrounding land is relatively flat. Hence, the word 'mount', for hill or small-mountain, and the name of the surveyor and first resident, Clemens, were combined into Mount Clemens. That's one story. Another is that he named his mapped out town after his house which he called 'Mount Clemens', such as 'Mount Vernon', the first United States President's famous home out east."

Heinrich continued, "Another story is he had difficulty mounting his horse after a day of taste testing his distillery product. So it was common to give him encouragement by shouting 'mount Clemens'." They all shared a laugh at that one.

The Woltmans shared some liquid refreshment, downing a number of tankards of local beer. It tasted a bit different than their homeland brew, but nonetheless accomplished the same end.

The Mallasts had successfully reached their destination conceived a long time ago in far-off Germany. They had experienced so much so fast that their departure seemed years in the past. But they had done it. Here they hoped to settle and raise their family in a peaceful environment. They anticipated finding a farm to buy or rent with fertile soil and fresh water, in a moderate climate, in a countryside much like the one they had left, the major difference being no military conflict on the horizon.

CHAPTER SIX

THE MALLAST FAMILY

From left to right: Adolph, Adolphine, Rudolph (standing behind), August (seated), Bertha (front, standing, about five years old), Emilie (standing behind), Rose* (seated), Emil, (standing behind), Fred (seated)

*Notice Rose's hat. Ladies of German Prussian decent, circa 1926, wore hats that signified their marital and social status.

Mallast Family
in Michigan

The very next day, August and Rosina walked to the bank, intent on opening an account to deposit their remaining savings. They had asked the Woltmans about a bank in Mt. Clemens and the Woltmans had jumped at the chance to recommend a bank recently started by a fellow Prussian immigrant, Paul Ullrich.

"He was born in state of Hesse, which as you know was annexed by Prussia following the war with Austria, becoming part of the North German Confederation," said Heinrich Woltman. "He migrated in 1870, ran a successful clothing store, and just recently opened the Ullrich and Crocker Bank. It's a private bank but go there and tell them I recommend you and also, most important, that you are from Prussia. I'm sure Paul Ullrich will take you on as a depositor and maybe future loan customer."

August and Rosina walked to the bank next morning, since August wanted to safeguard their money as soon as possible. Besides, having an account and building a relationship with a bank would probably be useful in the future.

"Nice to meet you," Paul Ullrich told August and Rosina in German, likely to test their origin.

August told Paul their intentions and gave him a little background of their life in Werdum.

"I will be delighted to work with a former resident of Prussia. Welcome to the United States!" said the ebullient Mr. Ullrich. "Delighted to see another account and I hope we have many years of good business relations, August. Good luck and regards to your family. I will get you a German-speaking teller and he will set up a savings account for you."

August turned his back to the teller, faced a wall and removed his money belt from his opened shirt.

"Here it is," August said, "all our savings from our farm work in Prussia."

August kept a small amount out, $20.00 for the expected week's expenses, and deposited the remaining cash in the Ullrich-Crocker Bank of Mt. Clemens.

Both Rosina and August were asked to sign a savings agreement, which would also be used for signature verifications on any future withdrawals or transactions. The teller, a former German countryman, also suggested that Rosina consider "Americanizing" her name to Rose. Buoyed by their migration success and with August's concurrence, she agreed. For the first time ever, she signed her name "Rose." She would need to explain this to her children, but she believed they would happily concur with her decision.

The teller also noticed, in the listing of the children, the spelling of Emiel and Emielie. He suggested they consider "Americanizing" these names as well, to Emil and Emilie. They thanked him for the information but wanted to discuss this with both children. When doing so, both Emiel and Emielie thought a change to the new country spelling was good. August informed the teller during his next visit to the bank. "Hereafter it's Emilie and Emil," said August, spelling each name.

August and Rose were relieved to have their money secure, especially since they planned on venturing forth into the countryside in the near future. Having no firsthand knowledge about the peoples of 1880 Michigan and having seen the immigration center runners at work, they were cautious to the point of being concerned about robbery while looking at farmland in the remote countryside.

The Woltmans had suggested August visit the local saloon and talk with the bartender about farm prospects. August, taking his interpreter, Rudolph, did so the next afternoon. They found the saloon owner himself was tending the bar when they entered the popular gathering spot.

The bartender-owner introduced himself to August and Rudolph and quickly grasped the situation. Not speaking German, but having been in this situation a number of times previously, the owner looked over his patrons and enlisted the aid of a person who spoke German.

August, over a stein, through translators, made his request. He was looking for leads in renting or purchasing farmland on a time payment basis. The saloon owner took note of August's name and was very cooperative, well aware that his establishment was a convenient grapevine for spreading news and getting business done, albeit informally.

The saloon owner said he would mention the conversation to his nighttime bartender and also talk with some of the more frequent farmer patrons. He suggested August and Rudolph, who by this time were on their second steins, stop by in about a week to see if anything had popped up.

During the following days, some saloon patrons, as is frequently the case, willingly suggested possibilities. The night shift bartender gathered information as well.

The owner and his bartender passed on the suggestions that sounded promising to August and Rudolph, discussing the reliability of the people making them. Some of the suggestions, the bartenders thought, were more a product of the fine brew their customers had imbibed than bona fide possibilities. Most prospects were north or west of town, but one was east and adjacent to Lake St. Clair.

August's Prussian farm had been located in a river valley with ponds for livestock watering so he recognized the importance of a stream or pond on a farm. He reasoned the Lake St. Clair farm would be very good for livestock watering, even though they might need to lead the cows and horses to the lake each evening. Still, the other possibilities might also have fresh water, maybe located on the river flowing though Mt. Clemens.

"The proximity to a constant source of fresh water is a must for our farm," August told Rose and Rudolph.

August, Rose, and Rudolph rented a horse and carriage from the local livery stable and visited three farm properties in the following two days. They talked with the owners about renting or buying while Mrs. Woltman volunteered to watch the children during their search. Much to his chagrin, Adolph, the second oldest, was left behind to help supervise the youngsters.

They discussed the properties each evening with the family and decided to revisit the farm adjacent to Lake St. Clair for a second, more serious, look. The lake farm was located about five miles due east of Mt. Clemens. Although it wasn't directly on the lake, the lake was in sight of the farmhouse, less than a half mile away through the shoreline marsh.

The farm was about a mile west of a series of small sand islands jutting out into the lake. They were connected during low water years, which helped form a peninsula with a river flowing down its center, having an origin far back in the marsh. The marshland itself was very large, extending about three miles inland from the lake, even touching the farm property on the north and extending a short distance into the northeast corner of the farm.

A shallow stream cut through the marsh beginning just beyond the farm's northwest border. As it snaked its way through the wet marshland, it connected with tributaries that all flowed into an inland bay about a half mile in diameter. With substantially more water volume at that point, the sizeable outflow was a channel large enough to be called a river. The marshland water continued its course through marsh for another mile and finally past the sand islands and into the lake. The channel was suitably named the Black River since the sediments were from the muddy, mucky marsh bottom. It was black and rich, which supported plant life with miles of cattails and lesser water plants. This rich, mucky marshland was a spawning ground for numerous fish species, a breeding ground for wild ducks, and home for hundreds of muskrats and frogs.

The tributaries entering the bay had their origins further back in the marsh, draining spring floodwaters as well as underground seepage from the Clinton River about a mile to the north.

The soil closer to the river was porous, sandy, and mucky, so the Clinton River waters seeped through the sand into the shallow Black River tributaries. The Clinton was about 200 feet across as it flowed past the marshland and entered Lake St. Clair, about two miles to the northeast of the Black River outlet.

August and Rudolph, having lived in a river valley that contained some marshlands, recognized the benefit of living in a fertile water environment. They realized it offered a possible source of income from the sale of muskrat fur as well as clean dark meat to supplement their table fare.

Besides the muskrat meat, there would also be an abundance of frog legs, fish, and waterfowl, all of which would grace their farmhouse dinner table from time to time.

The murky water of the Black River, as it flowed into Lake St. Clair, was overpowered by the sheer volume of clear, cool water from three large northern lakes. Lake Huron to the immediate north was linked to lakes Michigan and Superior, all very large, deep lakes of about 200 to 400 miles in length and 50 to 100 miles in width. The water from the huge watersheds of these lakes all flowed downhill to the Atlantic Ocean through a large river that emptied into Lake St. Clair. A large river connected the southern end of Lake Huron with Lake St. Clair and was the conduit for all of the three upper Great Lakes as the waters rushed south, then east, finally exiting into the mighty Atlantic Ocean.

As the river waters rushed toward Lake St. Clair, they divided into three main channels; the North, Middle, and South Channels. The waters from two of these, the North and Middle Channels, flowed past the mouth of the Black River as they continued their southern journey into the Detroit River, right past the city's docks and into another Great Lake, called Lake Erie. The waters turned east at this point, plummeted over Niagara Falls, and poured into yet another Great Lake, Lake Ontario.

There they exited into a great seaway leading to the mighty Atlantic Ocean.

Thus, lake water adjacent to the farm, although downstream a mile or so from a river with dark rich waters, was heavily mixed with the clear, clean waters of the north.

The waters off the farm were crystal clear on calm days or days with offshore breezes. It was quite the reverse, however, when onshore breezes stirred up the sand bottom.

These interconnected lakes and rivers formed the main highway of commerce for the Midwest during the nineteenth century, although they were rivaled by the railroads during the latter half of the 1800s. Thus shipping farm products, especially grain, was possible from Chicago and Wisconsin to upper state New York, off-loaded and floated on barges down a canal dug from Lake Erie to the Hudson River. This canal was appropriately called the Erie Canal, and by connecting rivers and lakes along the way, it allowed grain from as far away as Chicago to reach New York City. Water transportation was the only means of moving goods and people to many remote towns of the north in the 1800s; it was, for many decades, the only practical means of connecting the large east coast cities with the bountiful harvests of the Midwest.

The Mallasts spotted many passenger and freight ships, sailing and steam driven, as they drove their rented horse carriage along the lake. They were struck by the scenic view on this sunny summer day; it seemed there was always a ship in sight, either headed north from Detroit connecting to ports on Lake Huron and Superior and even Lake Michigan, or headed south with saleable cargo from the northern ports.

The shipping channel was about five miles from the Black River, but some shallow draft ships were headed for the Clinton River and appeared much closer. Despite the distance, steam whistles could occasionally be heard as ships signaled each other in passing. This scenery and the sunny day added favorably to the Mallast's anticipation of becoming tenant farmers on a scenic lake in their new country.

As during their first visit, the wind was from the south, filling the air with the distinct pleasant odor of the lake, marsh, and sand beaches. More importantly, they were encouraged by the rich black soil they saw, which was nearly free of rocks and from which sprouted lush greenery with many hearty-appearing grasses, shrubs, and trees.

They also observed that the five farms they passed all had healthy-looking crops — golden wheat and oats, some already cut and stacked, and high, green corn stalks still in their growing stage.

They continued to be enamored by the beautiful lake scenery, the fresh lake smell, and the cool lake breeze. Even in the dead of summer, the lake breeze was cool. This did not go unnoticed by August, who had spent many hours working in hot fields on the Prussian farm.

Finally, they covered the five miles to their destination, the last farm along the Lake Road. They noticed the road took a sharp northerly bend ahead, away from the lake, as if to escape the water and marsh. They later found that it ran just east of the farm and connected to the north with the east end of a road running from the village of Mt. Clemens adjacent to the Clinton River. It ran eastward towards the lake but by practical necessity was stopped by the low-lying marshland about three miles from the lake. August turned the buggy into the farmyard.

Their second visit was a pleasant surprise to the owner, Noah Moore, who had spotted them while cutting wheat. He quickly stopped his field cutting and returned to the farmhouse, where he greeted his unexpected visitors warmly.

"Always nice to see people visit the farm," Noah said, knowing their second visit was more than a social call. He had been about to come in for his midday meal anyway, so the timing was good.

He offered them use of the outhouse, knowing they must have been on the road two hours or more. He showed them the outside wash basin and water and washed up with them, using his homemade soap. He then welcomed them into his kitchen for milk, bread, and jam. Noah knew, of course, that a second visit meant they were interested in the farm. He was mildly excited, but kept his emotions well hidden.

Unbeknownst to August, Noah Moore had a mortgage that was putting a big dent in his field crop profits. Farming was hard work and Noah was interested in hearing August's thoughts. Specifically, was he interested in buying the farm or renting it? If rental payments would offset his mortgage payments plus some profit to boot, Noah thought they might make a deal. He was more than interested. He could potentially retain the property in the long run and, in effect, have someone else doing the hard work with an annual profit to himself plus making his mortgage payments. A win-win situation, he thought.

Noah was very attentive when August began the discussion, with Rudolph's help, in broken English interspersed with German phrases and words. So as not to appear too interested and to gain some time to mull over the possibility, he suggested they might like to look over the fields and the house, barn, and outbuildings without him.

"Good idea," said August to Rudolph and Rose.

Noah had a $1,000.00 mortgage at 6%, payable in 1887, just five years away. He did some mental arithmetic while the Mallasts walked the fields and he ate his midday dinner. His mortgage payments with interest were $236.00 per year but he would expect a profit for taking the risk. Possibly raise it by about $7.00 per month he thought, maybe $90.00 per year to $326.00. He knew he needed to be clever and not disclose his thoughts about renting, but the thought of escaping from the farm chores and the isolated life at the lake farm, and, most importantly, getting some cash in hand, was too much for him. He would relish going from land poor to money rich, and he listened intently to August when the Mallasts returned from their inspection of the land and buildings.

"The farm is 40 acres," said Noah.

A manageable size, August thought, especially with two healthy, young adult sons to help.

"I'm told the land was surveyed and laid out by Aaron Greeley in July of 1810. His land plats of that area were of varying size with the largest a 1,100-acre plot of marshland adjacent to the lake and just east of my farm. It extends east along the lake for a few miles then north to the mouth of the Huron River. It's still referred to as the Huron River by many of the local settlers but was renamed the Clinton River in 1824," said Noah.

"Most of the Greeley plats were in the 180-acre range while the plat containing this farm was one of Greeley's largest at

372 acres. It was conferred to a Joseph Campau, the owner of the 1,100-acre marshland parcel," continued Noah. He thought the Mallasts, fresh to the United States, would appreciate the background concerning the farm area.

"As the land developed," Noah went on, "the larger plats were typically split or divided further into smaller farmlands. The first farms were on or near the lake, usually narrow at the lake but running deep away from the lake so that more farms would have water access. In the early 1800s the lake served as a water highway, the only means of getting the farm harvest to market."

"My farm was originally part of public claim number 604, purchased from Joseph Campau in 1870 by a George Prentiss. It extends from the Huron River to Lake St. Clair, but I think Prentiss bought the land for speculation because he had it sub-divided. A surveyor, George Adair, in 1871, under the direction of George Prentiss, split public claim number 604 into nine farm parcels of about 40 acres each. I purchased two parcels before I bought this one in 1881 from a speculator named Rich Conner. Conner purchased three lots from Prentiss for $3,500.00 in 1877 but lost two of them in a sheriff's sale, sold to Paul Ullrich for a fraction of the original sale price. So that gives you some background on land deals in the United States," said Noah as he concluded his history lesson for the Mallasts.

August and Rose of course didn't comprehend much of what Noah said but Rudolph understood and said, "I'll explain later — it's interesting history of this property and how it came to be a farm."

Noah did not tell them he'd purchased an adjacent 40-acre property in 1875 for $600.00 but paid Mr. Conner $1,200.00 for the farmland. He'd probably paid too much for this land, since he'd later found out a 100-acre parcel on the Huron River sold for $1,200.00.

The Noah Moore farm ran about a half mile to the north, away from the lake, with the southern border beginning at the Lake Road. By 1875, roads connecting most villages and towns surrounding Detroit were in place. So farm harvests could be moved by horse and wagon to collection points in Detroit, there purchased by storage facilities for resale to local millers or resale to larger markets in the east, such as New York City.

Noah's farm was nearly 800 feet in width, with over 1,000 feet of road frontage running at a 45-degree angle to the north from west to east. The road bent in to stay on higher ground, out of the marsh, since the lake jutted toward the north a bit just east of the property.

"By the way, folks, my brother Frank Moore owns the farm across the road," Noah continued. "His property is larger, 73 acres, but it's next to the lake and about half is marshland and not farmable." He thought this would make the Mallasts more comfortable if they did rent his land.

"He would be one neighbor you would have," Noah said. "Even though he's my brother, he's a good guy and easy to get along with. So his farm is across the road towards the lake and the Villerot farm is next to you, to the west on this side of the road. Frank has been here a long, long time. The Villerots are more recent — a French family — and they are also very easy to get along with."

Noah assured August that the cattle and horses could be watered at the lake, along the east side of his brother's farm, where the land was vacant and mostly marsh. But Noah told the Mallasts a creek flowed not far from the north side of the farm, on vacant land that might provide easier access for watering. Also, the high water table enabled shallow wells to be dug, so water was plentiful at this farm. The land to the north of the farm, like that to the east, was not attractive for farming since about half of each was low marshland.

"The land beyond the woods runs north to the Huron River," said Noah. "Incidentally, the river is also known as the Clinton and probably the official name. The Villerots are a French farming family who have been using the Indian name for the river, Nottawasippee. God knows what that means, not me, but the Indians used that name so the French must have gone with it. Some information just in case you might get confused by all the river names you will hear."

As was typical for Michigan farms at that time, a few acres of woodland were preserved at the back of the cow pasture. This provided shade for the cows in really hot weather and much needed firewood for heat in the winter, as well as fuel for the cooking stove on a year-round basis.

A barn was about 100 feet behind the farmhouse, with a split-wood rail fence enclosing a barnyard. A split-log fence also defined a lane connecting the barnyard to the five-acre pasture.

"This fence is very important to keep the cows out of your corn and the neighbors' crops," Noah said.

Thus, with a few acres for buildings, the farm provided about 25 acres for cash crops, hay for winter livestock feed, and a garden for vegetables. There were also a few fruit trees that would yield tasty varieties for snacks, desserts, and canned fruit for the long winter months.

The house was of adequate size with a footprint about 30 by 40 feet. This included a kitchen, central room, and two bedrooms on the first floor. A large single room upstairs would be ample for the four boys. The three girls would be a bit cramped in one bedroom, but the twins would manage sharing the room with four-year-old Bertha. The central room was fairly large, about 15 by 20 feet, containing a metal heating stove and a fireplace. The kitchen contained a dinner table, some cupboards, and a nice wood stove with an oven. A shed off the back of the kitchen, toward the barn, would do nicely for storing firewood and frequently used tools.

August, Rose, and Rudolph had looked over the barn and two outbuildings used for chickens and pigs. A corncrib stood close to the barn. They walked down to the lake, following a foot trail they found through the marsh. They were quite satisfied with what they saw and returned to the farmhouse. After walking the fields and exchanging more pleasantries, August and Rose discussed their intent in broken English, with Rudolph doing a lot of interpreting for both his parents and Noah.

Noah had a rental price in mind, and they finally got to the question of renting and the key question of rental payments.

During his saloon visits, August had asked about rent payments from other farmers, so he had some idea of what to expect.

Noah started high and asked for $330.00 per year, anticipating some give and take. This would give him a profit of about $100.00 per year, equivalent to a full half year's pay at an industrial job and equivalent to more than a year's profit for many farmers.

August was non-committal at this point, but his brain was working. He wanted to look over the farm income records and take another look at the buildings and fields before jumping to a decision.

August asked Noah Moore how he sold his harvested grain and what prices he got for the wheat and corn, which were the prime crops he anticipated growing on a newly rented farm.

"I load the wagon early in the morning, even starting before dawn because it is a long, long day," responded Noah. "I take some food and a water jug and head along the lake to the town of Detroit. I figure it's about 20 miles and with a loaded wagon and two draw horses, it takes about six to seven hours to reach a grain elevator. Those are located close to the center of the town. I sell to the Union Railroad Elevator Company, about a mile past the center of Detroit. But there are a few others in that area. Once there, you will appreciate having someone with you to help you shovel the grain from the wagon. But an elevator company person will be there to lend a hand also. You need to always carry a canvas covering in case of rain. You don't want to get the wheat or oats wet, as you know from your German farming, or it will cause mildew and rot."

August pondered this for a while and asked Rudolph to tell him in German what he understood.

"Father, we need to take the grain by wagon to Detroit and sell to a railroad company," said Rudolph.

"That makes no sense — ask Noah if that's actually the case," said August.

"Mr. Moore, you mean we sell directly to a railroad, like buying a ticket to New York?" asked Rudolph.

"No, no; you don't understand. There are tall buildings along the Detroit River where your grain will be stored until the Union Elevator Company will resell it to local mills or to other elevator companies in Buffalo, or in large eastern cities, shipped by boat or sometimes by train. Finally the grain will be ground into flour at its final destination," said Noah.

"Your wagon will be weighed before and after shoveling the grain into the elevator receiving container. The difference in weight will determine how much money you will get for the grain. They'll take a few bushels of grain from your wagonload and weigh them. This will allow them, by using numbers, to determine how many bushels you delivered," Noah continued.

"But what is the basis for the amount of money we get for the wagonload?" asked Rudolph. Since he knew August couldn't follow Noah's explanation, he took over the questioning.

"You see, Rudolph and August," said Noah, "first they know the weight of grain you delivered by weighing the wagon before and after shoveling the grain off the wagon into the receiving bin. They determine how much a couple bushels of your specific grain weighs to obtain an average weight for your grain. So by using numbers, dividing the total weight of grain you delivered on the wagon by the average weight of a bushel of your grain, the elevator paymaster figures the equivalent number of bushels you delivered. The payment in the United States is by the bushel, so the current bushel price times the number of bushels you delivered gives the paymaster the amount of money you receive."

Noah continued with his description, relishing his unusual role as a teacher of the grain elevator transaction. "You'll learn soon enough and I'm sure you'll find the elevator system very interesting. You will shovel your grain into a pit where buckets attached to a long moving belt will scoop the grain out of the bin, lift it up to the top of the building, about 50 or 60 feet high, there to be dumped into tall, narrow holding bins. There are a number of these bins within the elevator building, which allows storing different types of grain awaiting sale. I'm told by the elevator people that the grain is usually shipped to New York City where it is sold to mills or transported up and down the coast to other large coastal cities."

Rudolph pondered the long explanation. It was more complicated than he'd expected. He said, "Mr. Moore, you lost me. I think all we need to know is how to get to the place where we can sell the grain. But in case we can rent your farm, would you please write down the name and location of that place?"

"Sure," said Noah, "and don't worry, you'll understand after your first or second trips to sell your wheat and corn."

"Oh, also you need to plan extra time when you take a wagon load of corn," he added. "The elevator folks need to get the kernels off the cobs, and they have a high volume corn sheller for that. You'll see it soon enough — two long tubes with a center screw, driven by steam at about 800 revolutions per minute! Quite a sight, so you've got some interesting times ahead.

"Sorry I got so long-winded," said Noah, "but it's a pretty slick system for moving grain to market, after you do the backbreaking work of harvesting and shoveling on and off the wagon. But the wagon trip to Detroit is restful, unless you get stuck on muddy roads or get into an unexpected blizzard or rainstorm."

Rudolph took time to give August a bit of the information, deciding it was too difficult to explain in detail, and he would see it firsthand soon enough, after a harvest. Then he said, "Father, I have the information about selling grain so we can talk about other things now."

August wasn't too anxious to leave the subject. "Hold on, Rudolph. I need to study Noah's sales records again and I need to know how much money this elevator man pays for grain."

Turning to Noah, August in broken English asked, "May I see your grain sales records, and let me ask, how many bushels of wheat and corn do you get in a normal year on your farm?"

August's brain cells were turning. He had asked the right questions to make an assessment of the yearly farm income from the chief source, grain sales from a 40-acre farm.

"August, you must realize there are good years and bad years in farming. This is no surprise since you farmed in Prussia for a number of years. The soil here is very rich, being in a river delta, but it is not very high above the lake level. So when it rains a lot, the fields get very wet, which cuts down on crop yield. I usually plant about 25 acres, most with wheat and corn, but once in a while some oats, because the horses like the oats. The elevator has been paying about 90 cents per bushel of wheat and about 35 cents for a bushel of corn."

August began to get cold feet because he though the selling price would be more in line with the selling price in Prussia. This was substantially lower but August didn't say anything to Noah; however, he would most certainly need to discuss this with Rose and his two oldest sons.

August, again in broken English, said, "Do all elevator companies pay the same, and does the price stay the same all year long?"

"No, August, the price may change during the year. I suppose it depends on how hungry the east coast is for bread during the year," Noah said with a smile, thinking his humor would be understood by the Mallasts. It wasn't, of course, being a very serious matter to them, but August took it in stride.

"Well, how many bushels do you get from the farm in a normal weather year?" August asked with emphasis.

Noah went to the cupboard and pulled out a well-used tablet, which he used to record farm sales. "Well, let's see. Let me add these sales up for last fall and winter. I had 15 acres of wheat and 10 acres of corn. The harvest was 285 bushels of wheat and 253 bushels of corn. Now, keep in mind, I used some of the wheat for chicken and turkey feed and a lot of corn for fattening the pigs. So the actual yield per acre is greater than the amount sold at the elevator company," said Noah. "I see by my records, the wheat sale was 207 bushels and corn was 35 bushels."

Rudolph wanted to make sure his father understood and took time to explain in German what Noah had said.

"I know, I know," the slightly irritated August told Rudolph.

"Mr. Moore," August said, "we have taken a lot of your time and you have given us detailed information, so now we need to return to the family and discuss this. We may return in a few days to talk further."

August was thinking that he would like to rent the farm but he needed to be convinced that they could at least make the rent payments. Above that, August's goal was to buy a farm of their own.

On the way to their carriage, August said out loud, "Can we do it? When we get back to the hotel, Rudolph, you and Adolph need to put your arithmetic to work and figure out our possible income for a year, based on Noah's sales figures. I'll give you the numbers, and you can double check with your memory of the conversation."

August was fearful the grain sales would not give them the $330.00 yearly rent Noah wanted. Before agreeing to rent the farm, he wanted to know where they stood. Would they have enough money to both rent the farm and save enough each year to buy a farm in the not-too-distant future?

The meeting with Noah Moore was very informative, August thought as he and Rose and Rudolph bounced along the dirt road that seemed more like a trail in some places. Nonetheless, he was very surprised at the low selling price of grain. It was much less than he'd been getting at the mill in Prussia.

Each of the threesome wanted to make a rent agreement and move to the farm, but the cautious August knew all too well they would have no other source of income except the money they could make off the lake farm. "If we can't come to an agreement soon, we'll have to move to a lower cost hotel or boarding house. The Capron Boarding House on Walnut Street rents rooms for $1.50 per week — much less than the Sherman House Hotel."

A couple of hours later, they arrived at the Brennan Livery and turned the horse and buggy over to the livery boy. August paid the bill and they headed off to the hotel, there to find the children giving their older brother, Adolph, a difficult time. Adolph hadn't allowed them outside even though it was a brilliant, warm day. Rose knew the children needed some outdoor time and took the youngest threesome, Fred, Emil, and Bertha, out for a walk to the river and its shady side setting. This soothed some ruffled feathers, and the twins decided to go along too, leaving August with Rudolph and Adolph, alone in the hotel rooms.

They had two adjoining rooms with a connecting door so August separated the boys, each to work independently.

"Now, here's the calculations needed," August told them. "I want you to each work separately, to see if you both come up with the same conclusion. You each need to determine if we can make a go of it at the lake farm."

"Here's what we know. It's 40 acres with the house, barn, and barnyard, chicken coops and pigpen, taking about five acres. There are three Jersey cows and two workhorses with about five acres of fenced pasture for the livestock, including a woods for livestock shade and wood for the stove and fireplace."

The brothers each wrote down the facts and Rudolph told Adolph, "One of the fields must be for hay to get the cows and horses through the winter, so that leaves the rest for the grain fields, our cash crops."

August reaffirmed that and told them that Noah averaged about 19 bushels of wheat per acre on the rich soil and about 25 bushels of corn per acre.

"Assume we will have 40 chickens and turkeys along with 10 pigs, plus a couple of big sows for breeding. The piglets will be fattened up on our corn harvest. We might get Noah to accept a lower rent, but let's plan on $320.00 per year in rent. The grain price here is much lower than the selling price we're used to in Prussia, so we can only plan on getting about 35 cents per bushel of corn and about 90 cents for wheat. We'll have household expenses for kitchen staples and a bottle or two of wine or beer for the special occasions and weekends.

"A couple words on milk sales, too," said August. "There are three Jersey cows in the barn and I know from the Prussian farm that we can get about three gallons per day from each cow. So if we use two gallons ourselves, we will have seven gallons of milk to sell each day. Jerseys give richer cream content milk and I heard at the saloon that the creamery pays three cents per gallon for Jersey milk."

Adolph said, before separating, "How about the grain for livestock and poultry, Father?"

August responded sternly. "You've both fed animals and chickens in Prussia. Put your thinking caps on and do the calculations. We need to know if we can pay Noah $320.00 each year and how much we'll have left over for savings to buy our own farm or to buy more animals for this one."

The difficult thing, August knew, was judging the intangibles. The grain harvests would be straightforward, but use of grain for the farm and the need to purchase necessary items, even food if they couldn't grow it all themselves, would affect the calculated profits or losses.

"I'm going to brew a cup of coffee while I think about this question," he said out loud. "How about a cup for each of you?"

Both said yes, and Adolph added, "Maybe it'll help us think, Father."

August said, "Don't forget about expenses when we take the grain to Detroit. Probably an overnight trip, and we have only two workhorses. Probably can pull about fifteen hundred pounds of grain each trip on the dirt tracked Lake Road."

August chuckled to himself. He knew they both wanted to move to the lake farm so they'd work the soft figures to make it

114

happen, assuming the results would be close to breaking even. Having a stake in the decision would also make them more aware of the need to economize.

"Write all your assumptions down," said August, "so we can compare the two results."

The hotel cook was tolerant of the Mallast clan and allowed August or Rose use of the kitchen for snacks and making coffee. The cook was fond of the children and enjoyed their company, at least so far during their short stay.

The coffee brewed, August mulled over the situation while he trudged up the stairs with a tray of three steaming cups.

"We really don't have a choice," he said quietly to himself. "We can't stay on at the hotel forever, eating into our savings, what's left of them, and we need to get started working soon if we're going to make a go of it here. Rudolph might be of help if he would work a job in the town — assuming he could get one."

He gave a cup to each of his sons, in separate rooms, and told them, "Let me know when you're finished and we'll compare results."

"Wow, Father. We're really not as well off with this farm as I thought. What about you Adolph?" Rudolph said as he entered the room Adolph was working in.

"Quiet, Rudolph! I'm still calculating!"

August took Rudolph's work as if he were a schoolteacher checking a student's homework. He could tell at once Rudolph had been as aggressive as he could be in siding toward the answer they all wanted, earning enough to make the rent payment with some small annual savings for a farm purchase. He waited until Adolph had finished and then critiqued Rudolph's result, which was barely over the assumed annual rental amount of $320.00.

"I hope you're right, Rudolph, but I think your $1.00 per week for purchases is optimistic — after all, we do like to have a few luxuries in life, such as tea and coffee and beer and desserts. And I must have tobacco for my thinking pipe. And your mother likes to bake with flour and sugar and we like her cakes and pies, so I think $1.00 is probably way too low. Also, the bushels of grain for farm use will be quite a bit more. But these are hard to estimate," August said tactfully to Rudolph.

"I think with some adjustments I just mentioned, your conclusion is that we might just make the yearly rental payment with not a lot to spare, if any at all," said August. "Do you agree, son?"

Rudolph had to agree, reluctantly and with some disappointment, since he'd thought the new land might allow more leisure time while not only making the yearly farm payment but also allowing some savings for purchase of their own land.

"Father, my calculations say the same thing — unfortunately," said Adolph, not anxious to have his father critique his aggressive assumptions.

August observed that Adolph had forgotten to subtract seed grain from the harvest and had the pigs and chickens on a starvation diet of one-half bushel of wheat per month for chickens and only one bushel of corn per week for the 10 pigs.

"We will have some skinny pigs," August said out loud, wanting to take some heat off Rudolph.

"Well, boys — that's kind of how I thought you'd come out. Seems there is always a need to work hard to achieve our objective — ours being to buy a farm in the not-too-distant future. Before I'm 80 years old anyway," August continued. "But you've identified some soft areas that we need to concentrate on if we're to make a go of it. Living as much as possible off the land and spending frugally on store-bought items."

"Another possibility is a job in town for one of you, returning on weekends to help on the farm. What do you think about that?"

August recognized the weeks working in New York blunted the edge on his suggestion. "Think about it," he said, adding, "We need to review this with your mother when she returns. I think she'll buy in so tomorrow morning, Rudolph, you and I need to talk with Mr. Ullrich at the bank about our situation and mainly his bank's financial backing before making this step. We have our savings in his bank and I have the letter from our Prussian landlord touting our good payment history. That should help in the discussion."

Rose returned without the children who were put under the twins' care while at the shady riverside. She was briefed by August and urged by Rudolph and Adolph to concur. Rose was more than anxious to get out of the hotel, being under constant pressure with the three younger children and the teenage girls. She jumped at the opportunity.

Adolph and Rose asked about attending the meeting. "I want to keep it to just Rudolph and myself to make the discussion more pointed with Paul Ullrich. We'll tell you all about it after we talk," August said.

After a good breakfast the next morning in the hotel dining room, August and Rudolph departed. August had another idea that he explained to Rudolph as they walked the short distance to the bank.

Paul Ullrich was talking to another person in his office as they entered. Explaining their visit to his secretary, she asked them to wait, telling them she didn't think it would be too long. The person left Mr. Ullrich's office, and they entered.

After pleasantries, August said they would like to discuss their farm situation.

"All right," said Paul. "Let's discuss in English since we both need to be conversant in our new language."

"All right," said August, "but I would like Rudolph to explain since he is more capable in English than I am and I too agree we need practice to continue to gain some command of the English language."

Rudolph summarized the situation with an emphasis on crop yields and their expected income being marginal — thus the future need for a line of credit or loan if they had a series of bad crop years.

August produced the good payment letter, which Paul Ullrich read carefully.

"Well, Mr. Mallast, I can't promise for sure that we would be able to loan you money if such ill fortune falls on you," he said, speaking in English, "but let me assure you, I'll do whatever I can to tide you over any rough times, but a lot will depend on how you manage this rental farm and your history of business dealings in this town."

August listened and Rudolph reiterated the content in German to make sure August understood.

"That's reasonable and we will work hard to make a go of it," said August. "Now let me ask a question. The price of grain is so much higher in Prussia than here. How can I sell my grain in Europe to get a much higher price?"

Paul Ullrich was impressed with the question and thought that August was an out-of-the-box thinker.

"No one has asked that question of me before, August, but it is a good one. Tell you what I'll do. I know a company in Detroit that specializes in grain buying and selling. A Mr. Frank Caughey is a co-owner of a firm called Caughey and Carran. They are grain commission merchants and might be able to help. I know Mr. Caughey and will write a letter of introduction for you so you might pursue your fascinating idea."

August didn't follow the details but got the sense that it would be worth pursuing and Rudolph reinforced that on the way back to the hotel.

Rose and Adolph were briefed, and they were happy to hear August state, "I'll buggy out to Noah's place tomorrow morning with Rudolph and make a counter offer of $300.00. Rose, if you will watch the children, that will give Adolph a chance to see the lake farm. Bring your calculations with us," he told the boys. "Those should help us to close the deal. If he accepts, we'll move in the next day if he has a place to stay. His brother lives across the Lake Road, so that might work out."

Adolph liked the farm a lot and this fueled the enthusiasm of his father and brother. They were anxious to settle in with a farm property and talked with Noah for some time. After studying the tabulated sales records again, August countered, which was not unexpected by Noah.

He said, "We have looked at two other farms but let me ask if you would consider $225.00 per year plus 20% of the farm profits?"

Noah knew auditing farm sales was complicated and that it would be difficult to substantiate exact amounts.

"How about $300.00 without the percent of profits?" he said with his previously thought-out counter offer. The profit of only $64.00 was much less than he'd hoped for, but for five years it was over $300.00. That was much more than a couple years' of farm profits, especially if there was bad weather.

The Woltmans had been very hospitable, offering frequent meals and friendly visits, but August recognized their hospitality was wearing a bit thinner with each passing day. Besides, they couldn't afford to stay indefinitely at the Sherman House, so even though the rent was more than he would have liked, he thought that accepting this offer was the thing to do. Again he stalled for time, wanting to talk with Rudolph and Adolph before saying yes.

"Let me discuss this," August told Noah. "Excuse us while we talk outside — come too Adolph."

They conferred outside and all agreed to accept Noah's asking rent. Noah was happy — he had financial relief and still maintained the property with an assured $64.00 profit each year.

A short while later, they sat at the kitchen table to write up a simple rental agreement, but Noah wanted a half-year's rent in advance.

This was an unwelcome twist for August, keenly aware their savings were getting dangerously low.

August was not comfortable with Noah's demand, but an idea sprang into his head as ideas sometimes do during the "fish or cut bait" part of negotiations.

Rudolph might be his factor of safety, he mused, in case crops failed or were below expectations. Outside again for a family discussion.

"Rudolph, if things get really tight, would you consider working a job in Mt. Clemens to help make the monthly payments?" August asked.

"Of course, Father," Rudolph responded immediately. "I can even start looking now" he said, "so that we might have a more leisurely farm start-up, without a lot of pressure to make the payments. That should preclude having to sell livestock or the need for a desperation loan if the harvests are poor some years."

Returning to the bargaining table, August told Noah they agreed.

"Next to work the details on the farm animals and poultry," August told Noah.

Noah agreed to accept three-quarters of any sale price for the chickens, pigs, and turkeys and to include the three Jersey cows, two sows, and the two draft horses with the farm. They would split the grain sales 50–50. They shook hands and both signed the agreement. Noah agreed to leave some of the furniture since he would temporarily move in with his brother across the Lake Road.

Rudolph was delighted also, since he saw this as an opportunity to exit farm life gracefully. He had enjoyed his work in New York City, and he especially liked associating with other people.

August wanted to move to the farm as soon as possible. This was fine with Noah, who would temporarily move in with his brother across the road.

"So much for the expectation of cheap land," August said later as they trotted off in their rented buggy. "The rent payment is more than I anticipated, but it is a unique setup and I think we will enjoy it," he concluded.

August suggested they stop at the saloon for a celebration tankard and to tell the saloon keeper the good news. Rudolph wasted no time in asking the barkeeper to keep an ear open for a possible job.

As the bartender poured the beer, he promised Rudolph he would do so, and to spread the word to the other patrons who offered suggestions as to rental farms. The happy Mallasts settled into a nearby table, toasting the decision, but not before visiting the rest rooms. They were delighted to have something to sink their teeth into, so to speak, with a farm of their own. They were also anxious to break the news to Rose and the rest of the family and to the Woltmans, who would feel a sense of relief that their days shepherding the Mallasts were over.

Sure enough, the family was ecstatic when August broke the news. The owner, Noah Moore, was happy per August and more importantly the Mallasts now had a home and a farm to work in their new land. Now, if only the weather, soil, and crops would cooperate.

August and Rose began packing the family up for the move the following day, withdrawing $150.00 to satisfy Noah's demand for a half-year's rent in advance. Rental agreement and payment receipt in hand, the Mallasts moved onto the lake farm, complete with livestock, poultry, and a resident dog named Duke.

The family was very happy, especially the five school-aged children, since, unlike Prussia, their schooling would now be at home with their loving mother as their teacher. And twenty-one-year-old Rudolph would have an opportunity to spread his wings by working and living in the village of Mt. Clemens, assuming he could find a job.

They had an idyllic setting for a farm alongside a scenic lake with a large waterfront marsh, 40 acres of rich soil, a woods for firewood, adjacent vacant land all around them except for two neighbors, both reportedly friendly, and a large, continuous marsh on the north and east encompassing a nearby creek.

August and Rose felt a deep, deep sense of satisfaction.

CHAPTER SEVEN

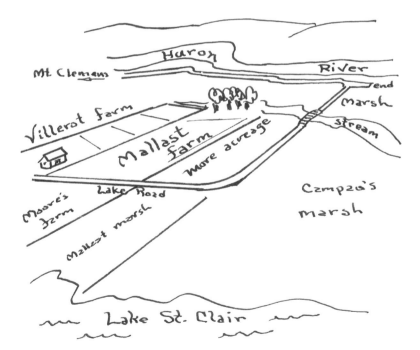

Expanded Acreage

The year 1882 was challenging and exciting for the Mallast family, having successfully migrated from Germany and rented a farm in Michigan. Quite a year! Once on the farm, they were immediately challenged since it was right in the middle of harvest time. The fields of wheat that Noah Moore, the farm owner, had planted needed to be harvested without delay for fear of possible summer rain damage. Noah had just started the wheat cutting when he'd agreed to rent the farm to the Mallast family, and he agreed to August's proposal of a 50–50 split on grain sales. He had done the planting, but the harvesting was also very labor intensive.

"From here on out, the crops are all ours," August stated emphatically to sons Rudolph and Adolph, as if declaring a victory of sorts.

August, Rudolph, and Adolph got their first taste of selling their farm grain to an elevator company in Detroit. They sold to the Commerical Elevator Company, almost at the center of Detroit and closer than the Union Railroad Elevator Company that Noah Moore had used. August was disappointed with the prices received, being much lower than the European prices he was accustomed to. He was anxious to pursue his quest of selling for higher prices in Europe and wrote to Mr. Caughey at the suggestion of Paul Ullrich, a co-founder of the Ullrich and Crocker Bank. Paul Ullrich had sent a letter of introduction to Caughey, asking him to accommodate a meeting with August.

August had followed up on Frank Ullrich's letter of introduction and arranged a meeting in late March, the year after arriving in the United States. So it was that August and his interpreter, son Rudolph, boarded the daily morning train to downtown Detroit. August was disappointed in the grain prices he'd received at the Commercial Grain Elevator near downtown Detroit. He was well aware that wheat prices in Europe were significantly higher than the $1.04 per bushel he'd received in Detroit. England was no longer producing enough wheat for their population so by necessity was importing large quantities, much of it from Germany and the Balkans. In Prussia, he'd received 7 German marks per bushel, and although the U.S. currency was still unfamiliar to him, with Rudolph's help, he knew 7 marks translated to about $1.75 per bushel. Easy to grasp that he would have gained 71 cents per bushel, and with the harvest of 200 bushels, that equated to $142.00 more than he'd received in Detroit, nearly one-half of the yearly rent!

August recalled the conversation he'd had with Paul Ullrich the previous summer, asking him about selling his grain in Europe. Ullrich had told August he wasn't familiar with the grain trade but knew a grain commissioner in Detroit by the name of Frank Caughey. Ullrich had met Caughey during a fishing day at the Denmarsh Hotel at the foot of the Clinton River on Lake St. Clair. Ullrich had been impressed by Caughey's catch of smallmouth bass and had struck up a conversation in the hopes of finding out what bait he was using as well as his obvious good fishing spots.

He'd failed to learn the fishing secrets, but Caughey had said, "I'm in the grain trade and have been for seven years. My office is in Detroit — a company named Caughey and Carran, Grain Commissioners." Ever mindful of banking interest in investments, Caughey had urged Ullrich, "Take my card; maybe you might be interested in investing in grain shipments someday."

As August and Rudolph had explained their quest of selling grain in Europe, Paul Ullrich had thought of the good bass fisherman he'd met at the outlet of the Clinton River. Ullrich had volunteered to write a letter to Caughey, introducing August as a potential customer, interested in shipping his grain to Europe.

Now, as August sat in Caughey's office, overlooking the Detroit River, he noticed sailing vessels dockside with tubes extending down from adjacent towers and directly into the bowels of the ships.

"Is that grain being loaded aboard ship, Mr. Caughey?" August asked, helped by Rudolph's interpretative skills.

"It is indeed, August — maybe some of your grain in the future?" Caughey asked.

August responded, "If that boat is headed to Europe, I certainly hope so. But that's why we're here. Is it possible that you can ship my grain to Europe from Detroit?"

"Well, yes, but it's not an easy situation and there are risks involved. Let me take time to explain how it works. Do you have about an hour before your train back to Mt. Clemens?"

August was thinking. If they did miss the train back, Adolph would have to do the milking, but he could do that. They only had three cows, so he could handle the chores by himself.

"Yes, Mr. Caughey. We will take the time, even if we do miss the train tonight."

"Let me start by saying the exporting of grain from the Great Lakes area is not a new idea. It started in 1857 as an experiment to determine if the lake schooners, with wind sails only, could endure the Atlantic Ocean weather. The first ship was the *Dean Richmond*, loaded with 15,000 bushels of wheat, that sailed to the head of Lake Erie, near Buffalo, through a canal to bypass a huge waterfall, into Lake Ontario, down the St. Lawrence river and across the Atlantic to the United Kingdom Port of Liverpool. Liverpool is the primary receiving port for England, with ships arriving daily not only from the United States but also from countries in Europe. And I was told the trip was very profitable." Frank Caughey paused to see if August or Rudolph had questions at this point.

Rudolph asked, "The ships below on the river today, are they going to Europe?"

"No, Rudolph and August, let me continue," Caughey replied. "The next vessel to sail directly to Europe with wheat was the schooner *Correspondent*, in 1858. The wheat was loaded right here on the Detroit River; 12,300 bushels. Wheat was selling here for 93 cents per bushel. What do you think they got in Liverpool?"

August ventured a guess based on his Prussian farm experience. "About 6 marks. What would that be in United States money, Rudolph?"

Rudolph did some mental calculations and came up with an answer. "About $1.50 a bushel."

"Can you believe it? They were paid $1.84 per bushel! Double the Detroit price!" said Frank Caughey.

August was able to follow the conversation and was outright gleeful at this point.

"This was reported in our Detroit newspaper, the *Detroit Free Press*," said Caughey.

"So why aren't those ships you see below sailing for Europe?" asked August.

Caughey continued, "Couple of reasons. Paul Ullrich said in his letter that you farmed in Prussia, so you know the risks associated with farm crops. You could have a good crop this year and a lousy crop next year. Or in other countries such as Russia or Germany, crops could be huge in a particular year, creating an overabundance of grain, driving down the market price. That's one reason — price fluctuation. You don't known your price until you tie up to the dock at Liverpool. The second reason is this area had an abundance of another cargo that was in demand in Europe, lumber. And its value didn't fluctuate nearly as much as grain."

"Okay," Caughey continued, "but before you plan on becoming extremely rich in a few years, let me lay out the whole story. The exports of grain, primarily to Europe, as reported by a publication called the *Chronicle*, were on an enormous scale which greatly influences the balance of payments in the U.S.' favor. Further, the business publication reports over two million bushel per year were being exported to Europe," he expounded.

"Now August and Rudolph, let me give you the down side. Just a few years ago a reputable concern, called the M. Waterman & Company, went belly up. That's a fisherman's term, August, for lost all their money. They did so on speculation that the Liverpool grain price would hold while their shipments of wheat traveled from New York to Liverpool. The price had fallen from

55 shillings per quarter weight to 25 — from about $1.70 per bushel to 70 cents. It's reported they had 30,000 tons of grain afloat, about 60 ships, which did them in with a loss of nearly a million dollars. So there is no price guarantee when the ship leaves the port. It's a gamble.

"Another factor," Caughey continued, "is the insurance covering your grain during transport. Marine insurance companies will only insure the grain based on the U.S. price, so you would be getting even less than the Detroit price since you will have paid for transport and storage to get the grain to the east coast. Further, as you can imagine, the cost of ocean insurance is about 10 times that of lake insurance."

August interrupted, speaking to Rudolph in German. "Ask Mr. Caughey this question, Rudolph. I am familiar with water shipping since the canal system is a big mover of goods in Prussia and throughout the German Empire. There are rarely any losses with these river barges. Isn't it unusual for ships to be lost or sunk in these lakes surrounding Michigan?"

Caughey responded to Rudolph. "Just about every week there are serious situations for lake freight vessels. Some are sunk and some are washed up on shoals, which could allow some grain to be saved. But sailing without insurance, if that's what you're getting to, is a very, very risky business, even for lake transport, much less the ocean."

He continued, "Let me trace how this whole system works here in the United States. First, of course, you deliver the grain, wheat or corn or oats, to a storage facility called an elevator. So named because it elevates the grain. It is done mechanically, with a steam engine driving a belt which has small buckets attached to it; each bucket scoops up grain from the receiving bin.

The bin is a big box-like container that contains the grain you have just shoveled from your wagon. Your wagon is weighed with and without the grain so the weight of the grain you deliver is known. You are paid by the bushel so the weight of a few bushels is taken to determine the equivalent number of bushels. When you sell in Detroit, as you know from your first year here, you are paid after all the grain is shoveled in the holding pit and the weight per bushel is determined. So you get your money at once.

"If you decide to sell in the Europe market, you will not be paid until the actual transaction takes place, about two months after delivering your grain to the elevator in Detroit. That is because of all the cost variables involved in the process. Do you understand Rudolph?"

"Yes, Mr. Caughey, but what are these variables? And can you give me typical costs for these? I'll explain later to my father."

Mr. Caughey nodded. "First expense is the grain commissioner, myself in this case, who coordinates the whole process starting with the Detroit elevator, arranging a lake vessel, which is less costly than shipping by train, to transport the grain to a storage port, usually Buffalo, New York. Grain is off loaded into another elevator at the end of lake travel, then a canal boat is used to move the grain to New York City. There is a man- made canal connecting Buffalo to the Hudson River which flows to New York City. A canal boat is pulled by a team of horses or mules or oxen, walking on a tow path built for that purpose. The animals are led by a person called a hoggee, usually a boy in his teens. At the Hudson River many canal boats are rafted together and pulled as a unit by a steamship, finally arriving at a New York City elevator to await loading onto an ocean-going ship, usually a steam propeller boat. Some is sold on the east coast but much is shipped to England, there to be unloaded and sold to a Liverpool grain company or millers. So you see, August and Rudolph, I need to coordinate a lot of transactions and arrange numerous contracts for all of these steps."

Rudolph repeated each step to Caughey from his note paper. "Now, how about the cost of each?" asked Rudolph.

"All of the costs I'm about to give you are in cents per bushel. Some will be only a penny per bushel but when taken all together, adding them up and when multiplied by the total number of bushels shipped, it will be a lot of money," said Caughey.

"All right, here goes. My fee is one cent per bushel, and each of the three elevators involved gets a cent so that's three cents per bushel. Lake vessel from Detroit to Buffalo is usually around two cents, while canal fee to New York is typically four cents, ocean shipping is running about eleven cents, and lake insurance is about two-tenths of one cent but with ocean insurance, it's about one cent.

"So all these expenses add up to 22 cents per bushel. Times 300 bushels, that's a big sum. It's $66.00 plus the risk of the Liverpool price being low when the ship arrives. So I recommend you think carefully before doing this, August."

Rudolph was busy writing down the expenses.

"What kind of price will we get in Liverpool and where is Liverpool?" Rudolph asked.

"Good questions, Rudolph. Liverpool is the main port for grain imports in England. And the price varies. Remember me telling you about the Waterman Company that went under primarily for that very reason? Right now, based on our last sale, it would be $1.72 a bushel while, as you know from selling in Detroit last year, you got about $1.08 per bushel. So using those numbers as a guide, you have 64 cents difference but don't forget the 22 cents of expenses. Even so, if all transfers and shipping went all right, with 200 bushels, you would have an extra $84.00 by selling in Europe. A sizeable amount when you consider a hired hand would cost you that same amount for a whole farm year! But keep in mind all the numbers given are changeable, being influenced by supply and demand.

"And on top of that, the sale of corn in Europe is possible as well. Currently the Detroit gate price is hovering around 50 cents per bushel while the Liverpool price is 83 cents per bushel. You would have roughly the same expenses for corn as for wheat. So that will create some extra profit as well," Caughey said.

"Tell you what, August," Frank Caughey said, "take these numbers Rudolph wrote down and ponder whether you want to take the risk of a long string of operations, with potential problems and delayed payments, in exchange for the possibility of more profit. If you decide to do so, just write me a letter and I will give you a contact at the grain elevator I deal with. It's the Union Railway Elevator Company located on the river at the foot of 17th Street. It's a bit further south by about a mile from the Commercial Elevator you sold to last year. Mr. Dan Stewart and his sons are grain dealers at the elevator and will set up an account if you decide to deal with me in sale of your grain to Europe."

"So that's the story," Caughey said, "and tell Paul Ullrich he owes me a lunch next time I see him bass fishing — either this side of the lake at the Denmarsh Hotel or the Idlehour Hotel in the flats on Harsen's Island."

August promised to do so as he and Rudolph thanked Frank and walked bristly to the Grand Trunk train station, just managing to catch the evening run to Port Huron.

August was thinking during the train ride to Mt. Clemens that $80.00 per year extra profit and squeaking out another $40.00 from milk sales would give them a savings of $120.00 per year. He thought they would need about a thousand dollars saved before they could buy a farm of their own.

"Rudolph, I think it's worth the risk. Especially since we want to buy a farm of our own before I reach 80 years old," August said jokingly. "With $40.00 extra from milk sales, we can do it."

Rudolph wasn't convinced because he knew, from his calculations and being witness to the breakeven situation now, that $40.00 extra was not possible.

"Father, it's not possible," said Rudolph.

"Sure it is, Rudolph. By adding two more Jersey cows to the three we already have," August said assertively.

Poor Adolph, thought Rudolph.

"I plan to work in Mt. Clemens as soon as I can find a job," Rudolph said out loud. "This should help as a cushion against bad harvest years." He continued the thought process silently. This would leave the milking to Adolph all by himself unless Father pitched in. Maybe he'd do so until Emil got old enough.

August said, more to himself than to Rudolph, "We've laid everything on the line by migrating from Germany, so we shouldn't stop there. Not if we want to realize our dream for our Mallast family. Your help in working outside the farm is most important, Rudolph."

They needed to do a sharp pencil, careful study in making this decision, August thought to himself. Frank Caughey had pointed out some risk, so while their income could fluctuate, the yearly rent was fixed.

That next Sunday after a tasty midday meal of roast chicken, home-canned vegetables, and squash — all grown on the farm — along with an apple pie Rose made with the preciously stored apples, August informed Rudolph and Adolph they needed to make another calculation. This time to predict whether the farm was on a solid footing, enough to buy two Jersey cows to expand their three-head herd to five head. "Two more Jerseys should keep the Villerot bull busy all year," August said in a joking manner to Rudolph and Adolph. "When adding in the Villerot milkers, that bull better keep fit and healthy to keep all the cows in an annual calving state. Without that big guy, we'd be lucky to get enough milk for our morning coffee."

August was aware they could also use two more workhorses, especially for grain delivery, which would cut their 12 trips to the Detroit elevator by a half. They would be able to carry 50 bushels of wheat with a four-horse team, instead of 25 with a two-horse team. "But four draft horses would be a luxury we can't afford. Better to buy a gelding for the trips to town." August was speaking loud enough for Rose to hear, knowing she would appreciate a less time-consuming trip and a little more status with a carriage and gelding.

When Rose had cleared the kitchen table, August verbally went through the calculation input. "We have 40 acres of land. The house, barn, and other buildings as well as our big garden are on five acres," he said. "Five acres are for livestock hay and five acres are pasture and woods. Let's squeeze an acre from the barn area and one from the pasture. That will allow 17 acres of wheat and 10 acres of corn. Every dollar counts in our situation. We have gotten 19 bushels of wheat per acre and 25 bushels of corn per acre, but the farm's needs must be subtracted from the harvest amounts. For the wheat, I think we need 36 bushels of seed grain, four bushels a month for chicken and turkey grain in the winter, and much less for the warm months. Let's say one bushel a month for six months. And two bushels a month for the horses during the winter months — say 12 bushels."

The boys worked together to calculate how many bushels they had left to sell in Europe.

"Father, with 323 bushels harvested, 78 for farm use, that leaves 245 bushels for sale. Father, at a conservative Europe price of $1.50 per bushel, that's $314.00, when considering the transport cost to Europe. The milk profits will be a cushion and savings. We'll easily make the $320.00 farm payment," said Rudolph.

"That's great news," said Adolph. "We'll use the corn, pig, and poultry sales for savings," said Rudolph.

"We'll be able to buy a farm in no time without buying extra cows," the exuberant Adolph said.

August was quick to bring him back to reality. "Let's not get too excited, boys. Now, we have 10 acres of corn with a yield of 25 bushels per acre. Our 10 pigs will devour most of that during a year — I think we need to plan on four bushels per week even though we'll sell the shoats each fall and winter, because we've got to keep the two sows and the boar healthy. And grass feeding will help but don't forget we will need seed corn — those stalks don't spring up out of the ground on their own, you know," he said with emphasis. "And pigs need to be fattened for any significant profit," he continued to make his point.

Rudolph again took the lead. "All right, Father, the harvest would be 250 bushels. Seed corn of 6 bushels, including seagull losses, and 208 bushels for the pigs. That leaves only 36 bushels to sell. I see your point, Father; we're not in good shape after all. The corn sales would be only about $18.00."

Adolph, anxious to avoid more milking, attempted to counter Rudolph's apparent chagrin. "We still have pig and turkey sales for savings, assuming the chicken and egg sales will make enough to cover our weekly purchases."

"Good point," Rudolph said quickly, picking up on Adolph's lead. "We only need to buy a few items, such as coffee, sugar, and a bottle of wine or a few bottles of beer once in a while," continued Rudolph.

Adolph enthusiastically suggested, "So we won't have to add cows to the herd."

"No, no Adolph — that says we need to add two or even three cows to the herd so we can cover down years. The crop yield is a big variable and we need to be conservative," August stated emphatically.

"Let's do a more realistic assessment, boys," continued August. "We get about three gallons of milk per cow and we use two a day for ourselves. We are getting three cents a gallon at the creamery, so what does that bring in per week, boys?"

Adolph used pencil and paper and said rapidly, "That brings in $1.47 each week, $76.00 per year."

"I'm sure the chicken eggs will not cover household expenses, Adolph. You know your little brother Fritz likes his extra kitchen treats, such as cookies and cake. And if the Villerots visit us during the weekends, we should be prepared with a bottle of wine for the French family," said August. "And same for the Moores, except a stein of beer would be better for them."

August directed, "Let's do an estimate of our weekly expenses. And oh yes, don't forget the trips to Detroit with grain. We stay overnight and need to buy supper and breakfast plus stable fee for the horses."

"We need to buy sugar and flour for Rose's baking. We need coffee, as well as the tea that Rose likes. Don't forget salt, pepper, and seasoning, plus vinegar and potatoes when our supply runs out or starts to get rotten. I'd say well over a dollar per week, just for these few items. And I don't think we can be eating our poultry and livestock every day without buying some meat once in awhile. We also need kerosene for our lanterns and candles for nightlights."

The boys listened rather dejectedly while August continued. "So looks like at least two dollars a week," said August, "especially when you add in refreshments for neighborly visits."

"What is our annual income from grain if we sold in Detroit only?" August asked.

Rudolph did some figuring and came up with $260.00 for wheat and $18.00 for corn.

"So," August pushed to make a point for more cows, "we are short about $50.00 for the annual rent since milk sales will be needed to offset kitchen and unexpected farm expenses. Hopefully the milk, combined with poultry and pig sales, will keep our heads above water."

"I think we had better invest in two or three more Jersey cows," August said.

Rose was listening intently and chimed in. "Don't forget we need to buy shoes and clothes as the children grow. And we need a newspaper and a magazine once in a while, and for church collection when we attend. I think August is right. We're too close to the break-even point and weather could turn against us. And we do want to save to buy our own farm."

August solidified the decision. "Jerseys are my choice because their milk is rich with cream and we get more money for it. We can debate these numbers but clearly we would not be able to save anything, and would need to live very, very frugally to make ends meet with Detroit grain sales. I'm glad I thought of the Europe grain sale possibility and will write Mr. Caughey that we would like to sell in Liverpool. So with Europe grain sales and more cows, I think we can save substantially. Good work boys, and let's keep our ears open for Jersey cows."

Adolph thought, "I lost that one."

August thought, "I need to pass on Caughey's invitation to Paul Ullrich."

Rudolph thought, "I'm glad I won't be milking once I land a job in the village."

Rose thought, "Glad I stood up for the children. We can't live like paupers all our lives."

While Rudolph looked for a job in the village, Adolph embraced farm life. Hard working at 18, his body was developing rapidly into manhood under the backbreaking work of cutting and bundling corn and cutting and stacking wheat and oats.

In the spring of 1883, the local blacksmith, Julius Koehler, offered to take Rudolph on as an apprentice and a helper in building wagons and carriages. They had become acquainted at the local saloon, running into each other a few times during the winter. August and Adolph were happy for Rudolph, but they were also very happy he was on the farm to help with their first field harvest and grain sale trips to Detroit.

Shoveling wheat and oats from the barn granary onto their wagon, then shoveling grain off their wagon at the grain elevator, even with the help of an elevator hand, was energy sapping, and it was good to have Rudolph's help the first year; this job was better done with three backs and shovels than with two. Frequent trips were necessary to transport the grain to the elevator in Detroit, some 20 miles to the south. The trips started soon after fall harvesting was finished and continued throughout the fall and well into most of the winter, roads and weather permitting. Twelve trips in all.

Rudolph worked well with most and got along very well with Julius. He was a fast learner and could soon operate the bellows driven "blast" furnace used to heat the metal into a softer state. The blacksmith sometimes allowed Rudolph to beat the metal into the desired shape. In addition, he was kept busy helping to build new wagons and carriages for the local farmers and village residents. It was at the Koehler Carriage and Wagon Shop where Rudolph introduced his sister, Adolphine, to a young harness maker, Charles Birth. Phina would visit Rudolph at each town trip, in the hopes of seeing Charles. Charles too looked forward to Adolphine's visits and they soon developed a close friendship.

With the village surrounded by farms, there was usually a steady flow of work at the shop during spring through fall. Farm mechanization, in its infancy, had more than its fair share of failed parts, and these sometimes needed serious blacksmith repair. Frequent plow repair was also needed as a result of hitting the occasional field rock with the earth-cutting blade. Hay cutters also had their share of failures, both from rocks and excessive wear and fracture of reciprocating metal parts, which were far from metallurgically perfect. Rudolph's 60-cents-per-day pay came in handy in helping to meet the annual rent as well as some of the necessary farm expenses during the family's first few years on the farm.

As a result of Rudolph working and boarding in the village of Mt. Clemens, Adolph needed to carry more of the farm workload.

"Fred seems to like farming a lot," Adolph commented to August one day as they milked their six Jersey cows in the spring of 1884.

"He's only 10, but he pulls his weight doing his assigned jobs," August responded. He spoke loudly, knowing Emil was within earshot as he forked hay down from the loft.

"Emil works well too," August continued, "but he is more interested in mechanical things, right Emil? He likes to learn about the farm equipment and especially new machinery that would make our jobs easier."

August set his milk stool next to the adjacent cow and added, "Emil wants me to buy a threshing machine, but that's just too much money. They sell for nearly a whole year's rent, about $250.00. We'd have to get jobs from other farmers to pay for it and there is already a threshing machine in the area."

After a pause, August concluded, "So, Emil, you will just have to look into some other new equipment that's not so expensive and ambitious. You are an ambitious one, that's for sure."

Emil felt good, hearing his father's comments.

The next two years went well for grain sales in the United Kingdom. Extra profit was determined to be $98.00 for 1883 but only $59.00 for 1884 because of an overabundance of the wheat crops. The English price fell from $1.72 to $1.42 cents per bushel but Detroit gate prices fell also. They realized an extra profit by selling in Europe but the total wheat income reduced from $368.00 to $296.00 in 1884, and continued downward to a European low of $274.00 in 1887.

The three additional Jersey cows were now needed just to pay the rent since the wheat income continued in a downward spiral over several years. Continuing reduction of income from $75.00 to $100.00 per year was an unexpected shock to August. It seemed their dream of saving a $1,000.00 in 10 years was not possible.

More bad news. Their dream was hurt even further by the sinking of an ocean grain carrier, the *Gulf of Panama*. Their entire extra Europe profit and more went down with the ship since the coverage was at the lower U.S. grain price and, as Frank Caughey had warned, the expenses to get the grain to the harbor in New York were real and needed to be paid. Caughey's general letter to all his exporting farmers explained the situation. August was shocked as he perceived his dream of farm ownership slipping further and further away. Caughey did explain they were very lucky to get a settlement since the insurance company, Tokio Marine Insurance, was near insolvency but had enough reserves to pay the policyholders. Caughey explained in his letter that future insurance would be handled by an English company with a big presence in the Midwest, The British and Foreign Insurance Company.

They were really in tough times as the years rolled by. The weather continued on the wet side, about 15 inches more rainfall per year during most of the 80s, cutting the crop yields by about 10%. By 1887 they could not make the $300.00 rent payment with grain and milk income when figuring in the grain-sale trip expenses of approximately $70.00 each year. Luckily the extra cows were on hand to boost milk sales to cover weekly expenses. Rudolph was working in town and helped with loans at times — a good relief valve when dollars were really scarce. The Mallasts were living comfortably but with no significant savings in sight.

Despite the downturn trend in grain prices, the loss of an ocean carrier, and reduced yield due to wet weather, August and Rose had some good news to share with the family in 1886. At Monday night supper, when the entire family was seated for supper, August and Rose decided to announce the big news.

"Rudolph told us during last weekend's visit that he is getting married to a recently widowed beautiful woman named Hulda Steffens. She was widowed in 1882 when her husband, Edward, was killed suddenly and mysteriously, leaving her with five children. They lived on a 65 acre farm across the Huron River which was subsequently sold at auction for $4,000. Rudolph will have a lot of responsibility with five children but he has a good job and Hulda, being older with parenting experience should be a big help to him."

"Her family lives in the nearby village of Fraser about eight miles away. The Steffens are thinking of a wedding in Detroit, and since they are paying for the celebration, Rudolph is content with their plan. They are being married in St. John's Evangelical Church by a well known and long time pastor at St. John's, Charles Haass. The church is near downtown and a celebration is planned at the nearby Wabash Hotel. Rudolph said we'll need to take a horse drawn streetcar to the hotel and we'll stay overnight. It will be the highlight of the year and something we can all look forward to."

"So believe it or not, we need to plan a weekend away from the farm! I'll have to ask the Villerots if they would tend to the farm animals for a night while we celebrate Rudolph's marriage."

Rudolph was 24 already, thought August. Thank God he wasn't contending with the wars and conflicts he might have encountered in Europe.

The twins, now 18, eagerly anticipated a night of dancing and partying with some of the young men and women who would probably be attending the wedding reception.

"If the men don't dance with us, we'll twirl around and dance together," Emilie told her sister Adolphine.

"Men are so shy; I'll bet most girls will be dancing while the boys stand idle on the sidelines, wishing we would ask them to dance," returned Adolphine emphatically.

August and Rose listened to their daughters with silent amusement. Needless to say, the family looked forward to some social activity and a really good time later that summer. It would be the highlight of the year!

If lower grain prices weren't enough, two years later, in 1888, the farm owner, Noah Moore, visited the farm to talk with August and Rose. He was happy with the Mallasts' care of the farm and their payment history. They had made every yearly rent payment on time, with Rudolph's help in poor crop years. In bad weather years the milk and other sales, primarily pigs and poultry, would not have been enough to augment the low grain yields. Even money from miscellaneous sales of pigs, eggs, and muskrat pelts wasn't enough to make the annual rent payment. Rudolph had to come to their aid. Without Rudolph's help, August would have had to ask for loans from the Ullrich Bank. During tight times for everyone, August knew he could not be certain of getting a loan to tide them over, waiting for return of good years, with no assurance they would return. Getting a bank loan was no sure thing — it would be risky for Paul Ullrich to make. Quite possibly they could have lost their tenant farm.

Noah told August and Rose he wanted to sell the farm and wondered if they would be able to buy it. Again August was taken aback. As if falling grain prices weren't enough, he thought. August responded that they wanted to buy the farm but didn't have a lot saved as yet and profit was slim. He needed to continue to rent until they could somehow afford to buy.

"Can you continue to rent for a few more years?" August asked.

"No," said Noah. "I've paid off the original mortgage, thanks to your rental payments, but I need to sell the farm to raise money for a business venture. I don't want to remortgage because of risk involved with the lousy weather we're having and the downward spiral of grain prices. The risk is too great. I might get caught having to make farm mortgage payments with my cash tied up in the business venture."

August was thinking. He knew Adolph, now 23, would soon be thinking of working a farm of his own, and Emil and Fred were still teenagers. August knew increasing crop yield wasn't practical and wasn't an answer. At Emil's urging, they'd previously purchased a horse-drawn corn planter and a hay cutter, which had eaten most of their remaining savings.

August told Noah he very much hoped he could find an investor who would allow him to continue to rent, even if the payments increased somewhat.

As they continued to talk, August formulated a plan to himself. The teenagers would carry more and more of the workload as they grew in stature and strength. This and their record of successful farming over the last 5 years, making all their payments, although sometimes barely, could be sufficient to persuade a speculator to invest in the farm based on an annual rent profit and a handsome profit if they promised to buy the farm for cash in five years.

Good weather and returning decent crop yields should make for profitable farming in the next five years. They would find additional ways to live more frugally, along with growing even more of their daily food and hunting and fishing more frequently. With a much bigger garden and using more poultry, August optimistically thought they might be able to pull it off.

August decided to make the risky offer, sensing he didn't have time to ponder the situation based on Noah's almost stonewall stance. He told Noah he would agree to higher rent payments and, to help make the deal, he would agree to purchase the farm from an investor in five years, for cash.

Noah felt a loyalty to the Mallasts and turned down some offers by prospective farmers. He did find an investor, Pete Haller, who agreed to buy the property primarily based on August's agreement to pay higher rent and to buy the farm in five years for cash. August signed an agreement to purchase the farm in five years. Pete Haller, using the farm as collateral, gave the Ullrich bank a mortgage for $1,150 which he used to pay

Noah Moore for the farm. August would own the farm, in five years, if he could produce the cash.

All three parties were happy. Noah Moore had his cash. The investor, Pete Haller, had August's note of increased rental payments of $325.00 per year with an agreement to purchase the farm in five years. They agreed to a stipulation in the note that the five-year sale price be mutually agreed upon or be arbitrated by the Ullrich Bank if they could not agree. It carried a $300.00 cash penalty if the Mallasts should renege.

Deed in hand, Pete Haller visited the Mallast family late in 1888 to discuss the farm purchase in five years. Pete wanted to lock in a minimum price up front with the Mallasts. He had expectations of a fine profit on his investment risk and told August that he would seek a reasonable price, but with a profit, for the farm in five years' time. He would not agree to a land contract or time payments to buy, since he believed a bigger profit would be obtained as long as the rent payments took care of the mortgage payments.

"I want you to know early on that I will expect at least an annual return of 6% per year on the property during the five years," he told August. "I want to be clear about that so you can plan your savings accordingly and so we don't need to get the bank involved."

August was taken aback again, since he was hoping to purchase at close to Noah's sale price of $1,150.00. An annual 6% gain, he calculated in his head as they talked, would make the sale price over $1,400.00!

"Well, thanks for the information," August said, "but we may need the bank after all."

Pete decided to retreat gracefully and told August that he might have really good harvest years ahead. He said, "We'll see where you are in five years, August. Your farm might provide much better profits than you think."

As luck goes, the weather turned stormy in Michigan for the next two growing seasons, so crop yields were down considerably. Compounding this were good growing seasons on the western prairies and central United States, so grain prices did not increase as one would expect with a low crop yield. The quantity and quality were down in the states east of Chicago while prices remained relatively stagnant.

August began to really worry. The farm would need to produce a $325.00 profit each year just to meet Pete Haller's annual rent. To buy in five years at $1,400.00 would mean they needed an extra profit of nearly $300.00 per year. "I can't expect Paul's bank to write a mortgage with nothing down," lamented August.

The Mallasts had 27 of 40 acres planted with cash crops each year. Nine acres were required for hay and pasture and four acres for house, barn, outbuildings, and garden.

Typical harvests had been about 19 bushels of wheat or oats per acre and 25 bushels of corn per acre.

"The last two years averaged 12 bushels of wheat and oats and only 18 bushels of corn," August said to Adolph. "We barely make enough for the rental payments, even with the extra animal and poultry sales."

They were really in tough times in 1889 when they could not make the $325.00 rent payment with annual grain income. Luckily the extra cows were on hand, allowing them to barely pay the rent and to cover weekly expenses.

"We need to make $325.00 per year just for rent," August said. "Buying the property would require an additional profit of $300.00. Impossible to do," he confided to Rose and the eldest son still on the farm, Adolph. "We may even need Rudolph's help to just make the yearly rental payments," he added disappointedly.

As the year passed, Adolph recognized the deep disappointment his father felt. He knew his parents needed his help if they were to have the slightest chance of keeping the farm, not to mention buying it.

The only bright spot for August and Rose in 1889 was Adolphine's marriage to the young harness maker, Charles Birth. Pastor Hermann Gundert conducted the ceremony, in German as was the custom at the Mt. Clemens German Evangelical Protestant Church. Both families were members and could understand, although Phina softly translated for Charles, who was not as proficient in German. Although times were hard, August and Rose paid for a small celebration at the Biewer Saloon, close to the church and on the main street through town, Court Street. They also treated the couple to a night at the Osborne Hotel on the Clinton River at the high cost of $2.50 per night. Phina was delighted and their married life began. But August and Rose soon returned to reality with their farm ownership dreams seemingly not obtainable.

Adolph was well aware of his parent's plight and their deep disappointment but he had a plan.

First, despite thinking of marriage, he decided to stay on the lakeside farm for the next few years. He would stay and help his parents somehow make enough to either purchase from Haller or get a good enough showing to get a mortgage from the Ullrich Bank of up to $1,400.00. And he knew Rudolph, married and working in town, could help with loans at times — a good relief valve when dollars were really scarce — but was not in a position to loan them money for a farm purchase. He had family responsibilities.

Second, Adolph had devised a plan to increase the farm's profits by expanding their acreage. With his younger brothers, now teenagers, getting stronger by the year and Adolph working as well, the four men could handle more. Accordingly, Adolph had his eye on the vacant land to the east of their farm. It was about 70 acres, all vacant, but about half was not usable farmland. It was marshland, so he reasoned they should be able to agree on a very reasonable yearly rent payment with the owner, Lyman Avery.

Adolph happened to have talked with Lyman about his marshland during one of the owner's infrequent visits to his land. It was private claim number 151, running all the way from the Clinton River to Lake St. Clair. Lyman had told Adolph he had no immediate plans for the property, and Adolph had sensed during their happenstance meeting that the owner might consider renting.

Adolph gathered his arguments and proposed to his father that they rent the southern half of Private Claim 151. It was 70 acres, but he thought they might be able to rent the vacant land for a reasonable amount since about half of the land was marshland and not farmable. He made a proposal to his father that he meet with Lyman Avery to discuss the possibility of renting the land. Such a deal would nearly double the farmable acreage to about 75 acres. The additional grain yield should enable them to save significantly more, which would probably ensure them the ability to buy their existing rental farm per their promise to the investment speculator and their tenant farm owner, Pete Haller.

August, consistent with his approach to major decisions, told Adolph, "I'll consider your idea." That night he put an extra big load of tobacco in his long-stemmed pipe and mulled over Adolph's idea. He continued mulling and smoked a couple of thoughtful pipe loads over the next few days as he sat by the fireplace late in the evenings.

He had walked the property and concurred with Adolph that the northern half, about 35 acres of higher ground, was indeed farmable. But he thought Adolph would want to strike out on his own in a few years and get married, but that was an assumption. So he couldn't necessarily count on Adolph for the long haul, but Emil and Fred would be able to handle more and more and Fred really liked farming. Even so, he thought they would need some hired help at some point — maybe one or two men — to handle the expanded acreage.

Ultimately, August decided that Adolph's proposal was taking a risk but doable with the help of the entire family and hired help, which would probably be needed. Even Rudolph might pitch in on his off days, but August knew it wouldn't make his wife, Hulda, happy. But he was sure Rudolph would want to help if really needed. They would have more rent to pay and hired hands as well. But August reasoned they had to gamble to achieve their goal of farm ownership.

"We've got to do it," August said to his gelding, the substitute for his favorite Prussian horse, Wolfgang, as he fed the gelding a carrot. "It gives us some assurance that we can buy the farm in the promised five-year time period," he continued.

So August contacted Lyman Avery by letter and asked him to consider renting the southern half of the entire Private Claim 151.

"Maybe we'll have a chance to buy the farm after all!" he said out loud within earshot of Rose.

In 1890, August proposed a written rent agreement to Lyman, sealed with a handshake and August's promise to buy his property in five years or so, if it all worked out. He suggested a relatively low rental payment, supported by Adolph's comments at the meeting that half the property was unusable for farming since it was marshland.

"A rich marshland is good for muskrats but not for wheat," said August to Lyman Avery and further, "The fields are not cleared for planting and it isn't even fenced for livestock graz-ing." August continued forcefully, "Both are necessary before we can use the land."

The comments had their impact on Lyman. He agreed to rent for $100.00 per year. August was delighted and they shook hands to close the deal. Lyman and August had struck a deal with a handshake and August signed a short agreement for Lyman.

Adolph immediately fenced the northern boundary of the property, enclosing the higher ground furthest from the lake, which he instinctively knew was well suited for livestock grazing and growing cash crops.

The new acreage was adjacent to and east of their original farm, starting just north of the original farm and running south all the way to the lakefront. The southern half of Lyman Avery's claim number 151, laid out in 1810 by surveyor Aaron Greeley, was one mile in length and 600 feet wide.

Adolph's idea and August's initiative had nearly doubled their farmable acreage from 40 to 75 acres. It gave them 600 feet of lake frontage with undisputed lake access and 35 additional acres of marsh rich in muskrat pelts, fishponds, and waterfowl to grace their dinner table. This was also a handy plus for cattle and horse watering in case the shallow north marsh stream should dry up in hot summers. All this, along with the fun and recreation they would have playing in the shallow sand bottom at the lake frontage, helped them rationalize this move.

Adolph and August were excited, but Rose had her doubts. She feared the foursome would be hard pressed to handle the larger acreage especially since Fritz was only 16.

Indeed, as the 1891 planting season gave way to harvesting, Emil and Fred found themselves challenged beyond their years to work the much larger 75-acre farm. Adolph was now considering marriage himself and naturally wanted to start farming on his own when he married, but he was torn with a sense of responsibility. He compromised by continuing to work the lakeside farm but built a house on the property and began his married life in 1891. He still wanted to help his parents achieve their goal of owning their own farm, especially since the increased acreage was his idea. Maybe additional help was the answer?

CHAPTER EIGHT

THE FARM LIFE

The Mallasts moved into their tenant lakeside farm in the summer of 1882. August's plan for the farm was the same strategy he'd used in Prussia: field crops for major income supplemented with milk and egg sales plus miscellaneous income to make up any rent shortfalls. They still had some money they'd brought from Germany, which helped them get established on their lake farm. That money, along with Rudolph's blacksmith wages, allowed them to successfully complete the first few years of farming.

Likewise, expenses were held to a minimum by eating farm-grown food as well as fish, waterfowl, frog legs, and muskrat, all so abundant in the surrounding marshland.

The products of a large vegetable garden and some fruit trees made for delicious supplements to the homegrown beef, ham, chickens, and turkeys. Fruit from the orchard included apples, peaches, cherries, and pears picked by the twins, Emilie and Adolphine.

Rose and the twins canned the fruit and vegetables so the family could enjoy them in the dead of winter. Bertha was anxious to help with vegetable and fruit canning but was not allowed to do so until she grew older, since canning could cause serious burns. She felt the need to help, and so was assigned some lighter kitchen and household chores such as sweeping, cleaning tables, and making beds.

Abundant wild blackberries made for delicious snacks and also canned treats. Spreading homemade blackberry jam on freshly baked bread with lots of farm-made butter was a fine way to brighten up the cold, dark days of winter. Apples from the orchard were preserved for winter eating by wrapping each apple in newspaper, putting them in barrels, and storing the apple-filled barrels in a below ground fruit cellar.

After a few years, they bought three more milking cows, giving them six Jerseys, which precipitated the nickname "Jersey Farm." The Jersey cows gave rich milk, high in cream content, and drew top dollar at the Mt. Clemens Creamery where the milk was sold. The lakeside farmers teamed up to make pickups and deliver the milk to the creamery, each farmer taking a week at a time.

They usually had one or two veal calves and a heifer or two, complements of the Villerot's busy bull. Some sold for veal and a heifer or two fattened in the summer and sold in the fall or winter. They always had lots of poultry, and usually about 10 young pigs plus two sows and a boar. Of course, hay for livestock and grain for poultry and pigs was farm grown. Pigs were fed a "soup" of water, sometimes sour milk, mixed with farm corn and table scraps, supplemented by grazing in the pasture during summer.

The grain sales constituted the bulk of the farm income. Delivery trips to a Detroit grain elevator were spaced out over late fall and winter, necessitating a 40-mile round trip by horse and farm wagon. Time to load and unload the grain by shovel and trip time required staying overnight in Detroit, a two-day affair, about 12 times each year.

Frequent rain and winter snowstorms during the late fall and winter also were factors, both from the human exposure aspect and dirt roads that became impassible due to muddy conditions or high snow drifts on the wagon trails.

Eggs furnished a steady but much smaller income, while the periodic sale of poultry and muskrat hides was a welcome supplement to the income.

The plan had been successful in Prussia, and August had initially believed it would work on the Lake St. Clair farm as well. August and Rose made weekly horse and wagon supply runs to town, enabling them to catch up on the local news and deliver eggs and any orders for poultry. He was encouraged by local farmers he talked with. August always visited the saloon while Rose shopped for necessary household items. He had discussions with other farmers over a stein or two of beer, speaking in broken English, improving yearly, or German, based on whom he was talking with.

So while Rose was buying their "luxury" foodstuffs, things they couldn't grow on the farm, August was getting the lowdown on other farms and farmers' crop plans. Her purchases usually included sugar, salt, coffee, tea, flour, and any needed medicines or antiseptics.

But before leaving town, August would make sure he had a few bottles of refreshment for Saturday night visits from their neighbors, beer for the Moores and red wine for the French family, the Villerots. He also purchased tobacco for his thoughtful moments with his long-stemmed pipe during the week. He would reflect on his past war experiences in the Rogasen Regiment of the Prussian Army. And he would wonder how his favorite Prussian horse, Wolfgang, was doing. He enjoyed these solitary late evenings sitting by the glowing embers in the fireplace, relaxing and reflecting on past events and contemplating solutions to current problems. There was always much to ponder.

They also attended the German Evangelical Protestant Church in Mt. Clemens, typically on a monthly basis since the farm was quite remote. After the German language service was concluded, August would discuss farm strategies with other German farmers. They were able to converse more easily than when he spoke with the French and English farmers at the saloon, necessitating use of his broken English.

August and Adolph handled the fields, livestock, and repairs while Rose and the younger children tended the poultry, garden, and house chores. When they had time, Adolph, Fred, and Emil hunted the marsh and fished the lake, adding to the table fare and the family's income with the sale of muskrat pelts during the winter. Of course, they all enjoyed the lake swimming and playing in the lake during the hot summer evenings. It also served as a handy bathtub.

The neighboring Villerot's sons, Ernest and Lucien, taught the boys how to trap. This was done in winter, when the fur was thick and travel in a frozen swamp much easier. A piece of apple, carefully washed to remove human scent, was suspended on a stick over the below-water entrance to a muskrat's den. A foot trap was armed and set immediately below the apple, under the water. The muskrat, to reach the apple bait, was thus enticed into the foot trap. Emil or Fred would walk the trap line after night chores, retrieving the muskrats and skinning them in the barn. Each animal was carefully skinned from head to tail, being careful to avoid cutting any of the body hide or fur.

The resulting fur cylinder, with fur on the inside, was stretched over a shaped cedar shingle to dry. After drying and removing the shingle, the flat pelt was stacked with others to await sale. Whenever they accumulated a dozen or so pelts, they would take them on a grain run and sell them to a fur dealer in Detroit.

The Lake Road farmers also took turns, on a weekly basis, picking up and delivering milk daily to the Mt. Clemens Creamery Company on Market Street in the village.

After milking, the milk was stored in large cans and set in cold water to lower the milk temperature, keeping it cool while awaiting the daily pickup by the assigned neighbor. Of course, each fifth week, the Mallasts had the pickup duty. The collection route comprised the five farms along the lake, then on to the creamery either along the River Road or the Lake Road into Mt. Clemens. The route depended on where the pickup ended, i.e., at the east or west end of Lake Road. The metal milk cans had each farmer's name painted on the side so the creamery could keep tally of each farmer's quality, by cream content, and quantity by weight. The farmers were paid accordingly at the end of each month. The creamery would bottle the milk in quart glass jars with a recently developed and manufactured wire bale sealing top, sold door-to-door by delivery men from their horse-drawn milk wagons. Ice, harvested each winter from Lake St. Clair, was used to cool the milk at the creamery.

Harvesting the ice from the lake was a big effort. Teams of men would cut large blocks from the lake with long large handsaws.

The ice was first scored with horse-drawn platform knives to define block sizes and float channels. Then, using long coarse teeth saws, a channel was cut adjacent to the "block" areas and cleared of ice so that cut blocks could be floated to shore. The blocks, cut to about one by three feet, with ice thickness usually a foot or more, were floated to shore in the precut channels, pushed using long pike poles. Each block was then pulled out of the water using large tongs and pulled up a ramp to the bed of a sleigh.

Once loaded, a horse-drawn sleigh, similar to a field wagon, was driven about four miles to a storage icehouse in the village. The walls and ceiling of the icehouse were insulated with tightly packed straw and sawdust to preserve the lake water in its frozen state through the summer. The blocks were sold to the creamery to keep milk from spoiling and sold to individual families in five- or ten-pound chunks. These were used in home iceboxes to preserve perishables and add a welcome addition to summertime beverages.

The Mallasts cut their own ice from the lake, hauling large chunks back to the farm with their team of workhorses. They buried it on the shady side of the barn and covered the bottom of the pit with straw and the top with straw and any available sawdust under a covering canvas. This made excellent insulation, needed to keep the ice frozen as long as possible.

With luck, the ice would last through the summer, providing for cool storage of everyday food items and cool summertime drinks of water and cider, perhaps even hard cider.

The six Jersey cows were kept in the barn in stanchions during the winter. The number six Jersey was known for kicking, so the Mallast boys had to be on their guard when sitting on their milk stools and leaning against her.

Spring through fall, the cows and horses were kept outside in the pasture. Come milking time, the cows were corralled in the barnyard except in rainy weather, when they were herded into the barn and into their individual stanchions.

Adolph milked them until he convinced his father that the two younger boys, now in their late teens, should be assigned that duty. The argument was won based on sharing the workload.

Eggs were sold at the Osborne Hotel and Hoffman Boarding House as well as the Prignitz market during the family's weekly supply run. Eggs were collected daily from the nests in the chicken coop, and during the summer stored in a cool, dry fruit cellar in a wooden box cooled by lake ice. In addition to a steady income from the milk and eggs, the Mallasts sold chickens, ducks, and turkeys during the holidays as well as pigs in the fall and veal calves during the year. Occasionally one of the fattened heifers would replace a low volume milk cow, in turn being sold. Poultry was cleaned and plucked, while the other animals were usually slaughtered at the farm or delivered on hoof to the Breiling's or the Prignitz's meat market in the village, depending on the sale arrangement.

The wheat fields were planted in late fall, the oats in very early spring, followed by corn. Fields were prepared using a horse-pulled plow, followed by a horse-drawn metal frame with rotating metal disks that cut the soil into finer, smaller chunks. Then seedlings of wheat or oats, saved from the previous harvest, would be broadcast or thrown onto the soil by hand. This was followed by more disking in an attempt to hide the grain kernels from the hordes of hungry lake seagulls that descended after planting. This was the one significant disadvantage of living close to the lake.

Corn was initially planted with a hand-held device that both opened the plowed soil and dropped a kernel into the cavity.

A horse-drawn corn planter replaced the hand-held planter after a few years on the farm, again using grain saved from the previous fall's harvest. The machine was expensive, but Emil, always interested in mechanical devices, convinced his father to purchase the new fangled, work-saving machine. To his way of thinking, it beat inserting every kernel in the ground by a hand-held corn planter by a long, long ways.

The field crops were harvested at different times. The wheat and oats ripened first and were cut as soon as possible after reaching maturity. They were vulnerable to being damaged by heavy rain, which could beat the shafts to the ground, leaving them subject to dampness and rotting and nearly impossible to cut.

The upright shafts were cut manually by scythe, and in later years by a horse-drawn hay cutter that had reciprocating thin, flat blades pushing through clumps of hay or grain stalks that were captured in place by fixed stationary teeth on a long cutter arm.

The hay would be left lying on the ground in the field, soon to be raked into rows for drying. This was done over a few days, and hopefully without rain. Damp hay could get hot enough to ignite, so extra care was taken to ensure the rows in the field were completely dry before storing in the barn. When the barn could hold no more, the hay was piled outside but close to the barn for easier retrieval during winter livestock feeding.

Harvesting the grain was a different matter. The loose, freshly cut grain stalks were manually tied together in handful bunches, with about 10 bundles stacked together in the field, in a vertical fashion, similar to an Indian teepee. This was done soon after cutting to avoid ground rot. Interruption by rain was not a good thing and involved the additional work of turning the cut stalks so the groundside was exposed to the sun after the stormy weather disappeared. Fortunately, the rain would not affect the grain already tied and put in near vertical stacks since the kernels were encased and were well off the ground.

Corn ripened later, in early fall, and could remain standing in the field even in severe winter weather. It was cut by hand because the stalks were too large and tough for the rather delicate blades in the cutting mechanism of the horse-drawn hay cutter. The stalks were bundled and tied together, about six or eight stalks per bundle, then stacked with other bundles in teepee fashion and left in the field to be shucked at a later convenient time, usually in late fall.

The corn was shucked by hand in the field after cutting and stacking. This entailed stripping the ears from the stalks and removing the outer layer of foliage, called the husks. This left a golden ear of corn, kernels intact on the cob, ready for storage. The golden ears were then transported to the barn area and stored in a corncrib.

The crib was built to provide good ventilation with spacing between the horizontal wood siding boards and with a roof to keep water off the precious golden harvest. The sidewall gaps were as large as possible to allow air passage which prevented rotting, but sufficiently small to prevent the corn from falling out onto the ground.

The corn could be stored for long periods, allowing sale to a grain elevator or mill, at a later convenient time. The corn stalks, if not dried through, could be cut into smaller sections, stored in an enclosure to prevent drying, and used as supplemental livestock feed in the winter.

The young boys had fun with the corn teepees. They would play hide and seek in the fields, crawling inside a teepee to hide from each other. The teepees were also useful when the boys reached their teens and would hunt wild ducks feeding in the cornfields. The ducks would feed on corn kernels that separated from the ear during husking or the occasional ear that fell during cutting, bundling, and stalking. Such ears were typically retrieved, but some were always overlooked, especially those hiding under foliage.

The teenage boys, Emil and Fred, would put shovels of dirt alongside a teepee to simulate feeding ducks. The clumps of dirt would sometimes decoy ducks into landing to join "the flock," at which time Emil or Fred would try to shoot one or two with the family's Remington double barrel 12-gauge shotgun. As they aged, the boys carved a few crude duck decoys, which improved their hunting fun. Both methods were especially effective with snow on the ground, usually occurring before the winter freeze-up, at which time the ducks flew south to find open water. With luck, they would bag one or two for Sunday dinner. Fresh wild fowl, with homegrown canned vegetables from the garden, provided a culinary delight.

The Mallasts would deliver their grain, after fall harvest, one wagon at a time, to the Union Railroad Elevator Company on the Detroit River, about a mile past the center of Detroit. The ears of corn or grains of wheat would be shoveled into their specially prepared, leak-proof wagon bed and hauled to Detroit for sale. Sometimes road conditions or weather wouldn't allow wagon travel — winter snow drifts or wet fall rains could make the roads impassable. These factors made the timing of the trips a bit dicey. Dry dirt roads or frozen roads were both good, but one had to be vigilant regarding the weather before starting a two-day grain sale excursion.

Harvesting the wheat and oats was another matter. Initially, the beat and toss method was used. As was done in Prussia, kernels of grain were literally beaten off the shafts and the mixture tossed in the air to separate the chaff from the kernels. This was easier when some wind was blowing. When the threshing machine came onto the scene, harvesting required a team effort, but the machine was a boon to farmers.

It accomplished the previously very laborious work of separating the grain kernels from the shaft, replacing the flail technique of beating the kernels off the shaft and tossing the mixture in the air to allow the foliage to be blown away by the wind or by quick movement of the pan while still catching the kernels.

Threshing involved two massive pieces of equipment, a steam engine and a large, belt- driven shaking thresher unit. The machine was massive, requiring a team of workhorses to move each piece of equipment from farm to farm. It was both costly and heavy, not easily moved, so the owner would coordinate a harvest schedule with farmers along a route, working in series, from one farm to the next. The moving parts of the threshing machine's mechanical shaker were powered by a steam engine, with a pulley-belt drive to power the vibrating shaker-separator.

Threshing required lots of manpower to keep the machine fed with grain bundles; it was a big operation carried out by a team of neighboring farmers and friends.

The farmers along the lake would band together for threshing, starting at the west end of the Lake Road, proceeding to work at each farm along the way until they arrived at the last farm on the road, the Mallast's. The machine would usually be needed two or three days at each farm, depending on the number of acres of wheat or oats needed to be harvested. The farmers would come together after morning chores, driving their teams of horses and wagons to the threshing farm. Before arrival time, the machine owner would fire up the wood burning steam engine, and when the steam pressure was up, he was ready for the first bundles of grain to be thrown into the vibrating, noisy, massive machine.

A loading team was needed in the field to pitchfork the bundles of grain onto a horse-drawn wagon. Typically, as one was being loaded, another wagon was at the thresher being unloaded. The bundles of grain were pitchforked into the machine, while one or two other wagons were in transit to and from the field.

Thus, not only were neighboring farmers needed but so were their teams of workhorses. The farm family at the threshing location was responsible for providing food and drink for the big, midday meal. This was a big undertaking for the hosting farm wife, so the neighboring wives would pitch in and help prepare big noontime dinners for the hungry, thirsty workers. A cold beer, chilled with winter lake ice, was a most welcome beverage.

The machine would shake and beat the stalks, separating the grain kernels from the shaft and expelling each separately. The grain kernels were blown into a properly positioned wagon, while the stalk foliage, now straw, would be blown through a tube onto a pile about 20 or 30 feet away from the machine. The straw stack grew larger with each wagonload of wheat or oat bundles thrown into the machine. The machine would usually be located close to the barn, which allowed positioning the straw pile for shorter carries by pitchfork into the cow barn and chicken coops. The straw would be used during the winter months for livestock and poultry bedding.

The moving parts demanded lubrication to keep from over-heating, so diligence was needed. If the straw caught fire, it could be devastating, with flaming straw being blown directly onto a dry, freshly stacked straw pile. Such a catastrophe happened on the Beaufait farm situated on the north side of the Clinton River; lack of oiling resulted in a devastating fire that burned down their entire barn.

Even though straw piles were outside, the individual stems furnished a natural roof that protected against rain and snow and ensured dry straw underneath for animal bedding, poultry nests, and the floors of chicken coops. Barn storage for straw was not done, since the precious inside storage space was needed for storing hay, critical for winter livestock food.

The grain kernels were transported by wagon inside the barn and shoveled into a mouse-proof room called a granary. The farmers inspected the grain rooms rigorously before threshing and made them mouse proof by nailing small wooden boards or thin metal over any mouse holes found. Tin from canned goods, when available in later years, made an excellent material for such a purpose. The wheat and oats were of course threshed and stored separately. Then, like the corn, the grain was transported to a grain elevator for resale and distribution in Detroit and elsewhere, one wagonload at a time.

Straw bedding for animal and poultry became soiled rapidly. The poultry manure-straw mix was shoveled out and replaced on a weekly basis while cow and horse manure was shoveled out daily onto a manure pile immediately outside the barn. During the winter months, it was periodically spread on the fields to fertilize and rejuvenate the soil.

When warm weather returned and the grass had grown high enough for the cows and horses to eat it without pulling the grass roots from the ground, they were let out to pasture until the snows returned again the next winter.

The cows and horses were put into the rail-fenced pasture, connected to the barn by a rail-fenced lane, which paralleled the road running toward the river. The pasture was furthest from the barn, on the north end of the farm, with a small creek running though the adjacent marsh. By diverting the fence line to encompass part of the creek, livestock drinking water was handily available. The small creek could go dry in summers without much rain, so in this case the livestock were herded to the lake for watering at the end of the day. This beat hand pumping from the farm well, pail after pail, to water the livestock.

The grass was usually lush because of the rich soil, high water level, and sunny days, so the summer pasture was more than ample to sustain the livestock. Plus, the woods offered shade and some relief from the summer sun and heat. Sometimes, when the flies were especially aggressive, the cows and horses would get a reprieve from pestering flies by standing in the creek mud and water, whipping their tails though the air, causing the flying insects to stay their distance or at least have second thoughts about coming close.

The cows would graze during the day and were fetched for the evening milking by Fritz or Emil. Sometimes the cows would come down the lane on their own but occasionally they would stay in the woods, especially on very hot days, and would need to be herded out by Fritz or Emil.

The Jersey cows were milked each morning and evening, which relieved the pressure buildup in their milk bags that caused them discomfort. They were kept in the barnyard overnight but in rainy weather they were driven into the barn and put in their stanchions for milking. Each was milked by hand, starting in the early farm years by Adolph and Rudolph. August joined Adolph when Rudolph began working in Mt. Clemens. Emil and Fred took over when they were in their late teens, later joined by a hired hand.

Though the farm sat in a rich river delta and was fertilized with livestock and poultry manure, the cash crops were rotated with hay, field by field, to help soil revitalization. Enough grains and corn were kept to plant for the following year and to provide for poultry and pig feed.

August initially took Rudolf and Adolf with him on his grain sale trips to Detroit. The boys were a big help in shoveling the grain off the wagon, aided by an elevator shoveler. After a few trips, a routine was established and August decided the twosome could handle the job without him. Adolph was quite familiar with the routine, so when Rudolph moved to the village in 1883, eleven-year-old Emil began accompanying Adolph. No price negotiation was involved, since he was dealing with a grain commissioner with whom all Mallast grain would be exported.

Occasionally they took plucked and cleaned poultry for sale to meat markets at Detroit's Eastern Market. The Ernst Meat Market was one of their frequent sales points.

Farm work was hard. There were the everyday, year-round chores of milking, feeding, and caring for livestock and the annual big field jobs of plowing, planting, and harvesting. Each year all the fields were planted except one for hay.

Hay was cut first, before the grain fields. The cut hay was raked into rows, dried in the sun for a few days, and then pitchforked onto a wagon for hauling into the barn and storing for the winter livestock feed. Any remaining hay would be stacked outside when there was no more room inside. The high water table in the ground, the hot summer sun, the rich river delta soil, and ample rain made the grass virtually shoot up from the fertile soil, so hay was very abundant.

Life was good, and there seemed to be always an adventure around the corner. The big Tom turkeys would chase the little boys around the yard, so much so that it was sometimes an adventure to get to the outside toilet without being pecked at ferociously by a mean Tom turkey.

Rose was a good cook, mastering the large wood stove with a built-in baking oven. Sunday dinners were special and usually included a fresh chicken or duck or even a catch of tasty perch or walleye from the nearby lake. Regular church attendance was not practical due to the length of travel, but August and Rose made an effort for the family to attend the German Evangelical Protestant Church in Mount Clemens once every four Sundays. And, of course, they attended on Sundays during the holy seasons of Easter and Christmas.

Cutting firewood, cutting ice, repairing wood rail fences, slaughtering animals and poultry for sale, trapping muskrats in the winter, daily milking, picking up milk along the Lake Road and delivering it to the creamery every fifth week, planting and harvesting grain, then transporting their grain to the elevator, and harvesting vegetables and fruit all added up to lots of work and long days. Although tiring, it was satisfying and healthy and allowed the family to appreciate their rural, scenic setting.

Life was indeed very good!

CHAPTER NINE

George Anthony

Hired Farmhand

George Anthony was the fourth of eight children that his mother, Nancy Ann, delivered during her 22 years of marriage to Henry Anthony. George was born in 1867 on a farm in northern Ohio, outside the village of McClure in Henry County. The farm was nine miles east of Napoleon, the Henry County seat, and three miles south of the large Maumee River.

Henry and Nancy moved from Crawford County, Ohio to Henry County in 1864, joining forces with Nancy's sister and husband, Emanuel Light, to buy a 40 acre farm for $450. Henry bought out Emanuel for $200 within a year and farmed successfully until 1875, when he realized a large profit in sale of the farm to Barbara Waddell. The sale price was $2000, which gave Henry and Nancy sufficient down payment on a much larger farm near the village of Weston in the adjoining Wood County. It was one-eighth of a section of land, or 80 acres, for the large sum of $4,160.00. To put things into perspective, a typical year's wage for a high-paying industrial laborer was about $260.00 and annual farm profits of only $100.00 or less were not uncommon. George was eight years old.

Farming 80 acres and making mortgage payments was aggressively optimistic. Henry rationalized that his expectations were realistic in the long term, with the anticipation that his three sons, eight-year-old George and his two older brothers, eleven-year-old Joe and ten-year-old Charles, would be carrying more and more of the work load as time went on. Finally, as the boys aged, he could maintain the large acreage at less cost since the boys would replace hired farmhands. Henry knew when they reached their mid-teens, they would be able to carry a grown man's workload, negating the need to hire farmhands for planting and harvesting. The ever-optimistic Henry even bought a used horse-powered threshing machine to harvest their large acreage of wheat and oats. He had visions of not only harvesting his crops but hiring out to neighbors as well, to help pay for the expensive farm.

With this thought in mind, the family continued to grow. Following 1875 and the big farm purchase, Nancy and Henry were blessed with two more boys, Rolland and Otto.

As one can imagine, the Anthony finances were tight following the big 80-acre farm gamble in 1875. Annual mortgage payments were very high at $700.00 per year, and with wheat selling at 80 cents per bushel, a crop of 60 acres at 19 bushels per acre would be needed just to break even when factoring in grain for farm use and $2 per week for necessary town purchases. If the season was rainy or too dry or they couldn't get 60 acres planted or all harvested, there would be a shortfall. They wouldn't make it.

Such was the case a number of times as Henry had to periodically borrow money to make the mortgage payments and keep the farm running. He was a risk-taker who was not adverse to asking for help. Henry asked his father, William Anthony, a successful farmer a few counties away, for help. William still lived in Crawford County, Henry and Nancy's birthplace.

He did come to Henry's aid with a loan of $908.00. A financer, Mr. C. Call, also provided a loan, for $936.00. Henry kept the farm afloat, albeit barely, but he kept thinking that if he could hold on, help was on the way soon since his three oldest sons were getting bigger and stronger with each passing year.

George was just eight years old when he had his first taste of family tragedy. His baby sister, Flora, died an infant before her second birthday. Five years later tragedy struck again.

Typhoid fever struck the Anthony family with a vengeance in the later half of 1879, claiming George's father and his ten-year-old sister, Mary Eva, before the New Year struck. His mother and baby brother was also taken very seriously ill but fortunately, they survived. Speculation was that a tainted well was the cause of the typhoid breakout.

Struck with grief following the death of her husband and daughter, Nancy, although unable to read or write, bravely petitioned the probate court to become administrator of the estate — an estate that was land rich but money poor. The daily farm operation was now entirely on the backs of the three teen-age sons, Joe, the oldest at 16, Charles at 14, and George, the youngest at 12. They were immediately thrust into the formidable task of running an 80-acre family farm in the fall of 1879. Fortunately, they had a few months' breathing room since the crops had been harvested and the winter wheat had been planted.

The family struggled on. Three teenagers managed to keep the farm going while their mother decided what their next step would be. She put Joe in charge with Charles and George as young laborers.

They managed as best they could. Daily chores were doable but with 10 acres of corn to plant in the spring, followed by cutting five acres of hay, then harvesting 60 acres of wheat in the summer, followed by 10 acres of corn in the fall, while maintaining daily chores, was an impossible task for the three teenagers to handle.

But all this and more was necessary to continue farm life and to make the annual mortgage payment.

Nancy knew her sons could handle the daily chores but she watched as the boys struggled in the following year to cope with their challenge of field crops. Down deep, she knew they would need hired help and it was soon apparent they truly did need more manpower to manage the large acreage. She would have to hire help for spring planting, and these hired help expenses would make the annual mortgage payments even more diffi-cult than they had been. During the spring planting season she clearly saw the impossibility of the task. The boys were just too young to make a go of the large farm her ambitious husband had bought. It was a catch-22: the hired help was essential to keep the farm operating, but the hired help expenses ate into the profits so mortgage payments could not be made in full.

She sadly realized she would have to shut the farm down and liquidate the equipment, stock, and some land in order to gather as much cash as possible in an attempt to pay the estate creditors. Although the creditors were generally patient, she recognized the responsibility to repay as many as possible in a timely basis. She held a farm auction that was well attended.

The farm animals, equipment, and anything of value was auctioned off in an attempt to pay claims against the estate — most formidable were the repayment of loans taken by Henry to keep the farm from foreclosure. She was even able to sell the used horse powered threshing machine to her son-in-law, Laura Della's husband, William Baumgartner, for $25.00. The auction raised a little over $1,000.00, which was a sizeable amount but far from enough to pay all of the creditors.

There was a long list of creditors, 22 of whom received some payment by Nancy following the auction. Payments to individual lenders ranged from $99.00 to A. V. Wade to $37.00 for William Baumgardener. Individual debts of needed farm services ranged from $1.50 for the blacksmith to $6.00 for the saw man. Shoes were $2.50. Farm help was $7.00, probate and attorney $13.00, while the medical pain killer man was paid $3.00. In addition, Nancy kept the farm payments current with two payments to E. W. Merry totaling $868.00.

Nancy was taking hold of the situation during the year following Henry's death when tragedy struck again. George and siblings would again experience a trauma to remember their entire lives.

Only a little more than a year after Henry's death, on Christmas night, a fire broke out unnoticed in the kitchen of their two-story pine-frame house.

Nancy faced terror as she opened the kitchen door and was greeted by bellowing smoke and flames. The kitchen with its wood stove was engulfed. All the children were asleep upstairs except for baby Otto, asleep in Nancy's downstairs bedroom. The front door was locked with the key in the kitchen, impossible to reach. Nancy grabbed Otto, kicked out a glass pane, and gently threw him outside. Hollering upstairs, Joe awoke and grabbed three-year-old Rollie and managed to run downstairs through the flames while hollering to his brothers and visiting young niece to get out. The stairs were engulfed by this time. Joe and Nancy threw themselves, Rolland in Joe's arms, through the broken glass window to safety outside. Nancy, severely burned, hollered frantically, almost hysterically, for the children to jump out the second-story window. George did jump but Charles and niece Mary, probably in a daze, did not. They both perished in the fire.

Donations were called for in Nancy's hometown in Crawford County and neighbors helped them through the ensuing months.

Nancy, although severely burned in the fire, recovered with time and continued her duties as administrator of the estate. She had done well so far, despite the lack of reading and writing skills. She was able to obtain a dower from probate court that gave her enough money from the estate for living expenses for herself and her children.

George observed all these maneuverings as he grew into his upper teen years. He knew there were still creditors to pay but with no money he recognized his mother's only choice now was to liquidate the farm property. Not an easy task with no ready buyers in sight. However, she skillfully maneuvered her way through this hurdle, first selling 19 acres in 1882 to her father-in-law, William Anthony. She had to obtain probate court approval for the land sale, which she applied for and got. Nineteen acres and buildings were sold to William Anthony for $1,100.00. So with the land sale proceeds and the previous farm auction, Nancy accumulated enough money to pay for many but not all of the claims against the estate. Still, this gave her some breathing room until she figured out her next step.

Three years after her husband's death, in 1882, she still had outstanding claims of $750.00 with absolutely no assets left except the remaining 60 acres of farm property. She sadly recognized the remaining land would need to be sold.

At this point two things happened. First Nancy, knowing she had to sell all of the remaining property, began the sales process. The court ordered an appraisal of the remaining 60 acres of farmland, which came in at $3,000.00. This delighted Nancy, since all creditors would be paid in full and a handsome amount would be left for inheritance payments to each of the surviving children. But first, she had to convert the land into cash.

She placed sale notices in the Wood County Sentinel and the adjacent county newspaper, the Putnam County Sentinel. In addition, she asked everyone she came in contact with to spread the word in hopes of finding a buyer. But there were no buyers — $3,000.00 was a tremendous amount of money for most people in 1882. She was downtrodden. What to do now?

The second event, in effect, led to an answer for her question. A successful farmer in a neighboring section, William Houston, began courting Nancy in 1882. William had financial success in Perrysburg, owning and operating a Dry Goods Store on Front Street for 15 years, starting at the age of 19 in 1851. He sold in 1866 along with his numerous town lots purchased for speculation and moved to the Weston area. Nancy had known William for many years, being farmers in relative close proximity, and they married soon after the courtship started. This gave her standing in the community and especially at the bank since William had financial success. It also provided an adult confidant and partner who could understand her situation, her disappointments, and help derive possible solutions.

She realized the estate was complex. Not only because the remaining asset was land, difficult to convert to cash, but equally challenging was the fact that four of the five children heirs were minors. The probate judge told her the underage children would need a court-appointed guardian to protect and manage their inheritance until each reached the age of 21. Nancy did some mental calculating and realized the estate settlement date was 17 years down the road since her youngest child, Otto, was only a baby at Henry's death.

Nancy and William discussed the situation a number of times in great detail and decided on a strategy.

Based on the property not selling initially, they settled on a course of action that might, they thought, allow the estate to be settled and allow Nancy to preserve the property in her name. First step was to ask the probate court to appoint another person to be administrator of the estate.

This was done, and the newly appointed administrator, George W. Will, soon recognized he had the task of liquidating the only remaining asset, the farm property. He petitioned the court to sell the property. The court needed the landowner's concurrence for sale of the property and, of course, Nancy concurred. Being unable to write, she made her mark in lieu of a signature. She vacated her dower interest (her support income from the estate, for living expenses), being advised this would simplify the sale of the property.

She had done amazingly well as administrator, navigating through the complexities of the probate court without being able to read or write. She could now relax somewhat with estate responsibilities being carried out by the legal system of Ohio.

The court ordered a private sale, but after a few months of further advertising there were no potential buyers in sight. Not a surprise to Nancy and William. The administrator, George Will, asked the court to change its order to a sheriff's sale, in effect a public auction.

Nancy, now Nancy Houston, made a bid of $3,000.00 at the public sale in 1883. There were no other bidders in sight, so Nancy, with her husband's financial backing, was awarded the property for $3,000.00. The sale was final. She had legally purchased the property from the estate.

George Will, the administrator, conveyed a deed to Nancy stipulating immediate payment of $1,000.00 to the estate with the same amount due each year thereafter for two years. The payments were supported by William, her second husband, allowing a rather clever solution to the property liquidity problem of the Henry Anthony Estate.

Thus, she was the recipient of the 60 acres for one-half of the $3,000.00 sale price, since as wife of the deceased, she was awarded half of the estate value. In effect she re-procured 60 acres of the original 80-acre farm for half the price. Her husband put up the money, essentially $1,500.00 in total, to satisfy the court's conditions for sale. Had she remained administrator, likely she would not have been allowed to auction the farmland *and* sell it to herself. A brilliant move, all things above-board and legal.

A year later, for $937.00, she repurchased the 19 acres she'd sold to her father-in-law. This took quite a while and required many moves with the probate court, but she retained all 80 acres (minus one acre sold to the school board by Henry before his death) of the original Anthony farm. So the original 80-acre farm was back together and the four underage sons would have living expenses and substantial remaining lump sum inheritances. Each would be paid when they reached 21 years of age, all managed by the court-appointed estate administrator George W. Will.

George, 12 years old at the start of all this, was now 16 and his older brother Joe was 19. His mother's remarriage was of course a very significant event in young George's life. His stepfather essentially took over the Anthony farm after it was resurrected, albeit at arm's length. The teenage boys were put back to work under the guidance of their new "father," William Houston. Their stepfather had farm property of his own, but unselfishly took on the additional responsibility of overseeing the Anthony farm and naturally assigned the oldest son, Joe, to be the person in charge.

This left George working for his older brother. He was not a happy camper but nonetheless pitched in and worked with Joe, his senior by just four years. They hired additional help and managed the farm helped by their father-in-law's suggestions and direction. Settling the estate was complicated and George was very sympathetic to his mother's effort to reunite the homestead, but by the same token, he recognized very quickly that he didn't want to work for his brother all his life.

George accepted his role but did not always agree with his stepfather's planning decisions. Being an independent thinker, he certainly did not agree with many of his brother's daily orders. As time went on, he continued to be more and more convinced that working the family farm was not going to be his life's work, especially under his older brother. George was tolerant and recognized William was trying to help their situation, but when the time came, he was determined to strike out on his own. Nonetheless, he got to know his stepfather from a farm laborer-to-owner relationship and developed a fondness for his new "father."

George decided, in the youthful exuberance of 16, that he would move out after getting his inheritance at 21. He wanted to own his own farm someday. George reasoned that his prominent father-in-law would be on the scene along with brother Joe to carry on with the Anthony farm. He would miss the family but would have no feelings of guilt in leaving his mother, stepfather, and older brother to cope with the 80-acre farm without him. His mother had two pre-teen sons to raise and George's sister, Laura Della, was married and living in the area, so his mother would be very well occupied. Such a situation gave him the opportunity to gracefully strike out on his own. But most importantly, it allowed him to escape his older brother's daily directives. He waited for his opportunity.

The Anthony farm was near a small village of Weston, in north-central Ohio. There were very few jobs available in the village so George's options were to continue working seasonally as a farm laborer or to move to a large city to find a steady paying, year-round job. Steady work would allow him to systematically save for a farm of his own and allow savings at a faster pace than working seasonal jobs. And moving off the farm to a city would allow him more individual freedom to spread his wings. His goals in mind at a young age, he definitely decided to move after 21 and find a steady paying job to realize his expectations of owning his own farm

As George neared high school graduation in 1885, he thought more and more of what jobs he could get. Finally he talked with his mother Nancy during the following summer.

"Mother, I've been thinking about working on our farm with my brother Joe but he's older and would always want to be boss. Plus the farm would need to support the family and if Joe married, the farm would need to support two families."

Nancy knew where this was headed and of course wanted to keep George close to home. "Well, beloved son, you need to decide that question for yourself but don't forget my husband has a farm as well. I'm sure he would welcome you as an apprentice on his farm. You could probably live there as well, since William has moved in with us."

"But I would still be second fiddle. I guess learning for a few years wouldn't be too bad and maybe the estate inheritance will give me enough to buy a farm of my own. That's what I really want," countered George.

"George," said Nancy, "your inheritance won't be nearly enough to do that. Why don't you ask the estate administrator to give you an estimate of the money you will receive. And, don't forget, you won't get that money until you're 21. A few years away."

"True. Farming is about the only job around here, and I don't have any money to move out after graduation, to start looking for a job in Napoleon or Bowling Green."

Nancy's husband, William, came into the kitchen and soon caught the drift of the conversation. He was essentially running two farms and had definite ideas about what George should be doing.

"You need to work with Joe on your mother's farm after graduation, George," he said in no uncertain terms. "Joe is still learning and needs all the help he can get — so you're it! It's a matter of keeping food on the table and the mortgage payment made on time."

George was still not comfortable with his stepfather and knew it was time to close the conversation.

"Guess I have no choice," responded George. "But I know Joe and I will have our differences, so I think you should decide who's right when we can't agree," he courageously said to this stepfather, William.

William's face flushed and George prepared himself for a strong rebuttal, which came forthwith.

"Listen, George, Joe is the oldest and has more experience than you. He's your boss. So I don't want to hear of any frivolous arguments! You two had better figure out how to resolve your differences on your own."

George knew the conversation was over but he wanted a way to end it and still keep on reasonably good terms with his stepfather.

"I'll do my share," was all that George could think of.

William was calmer now and had come in from the fields for the midday meal.

"I'll see what Joe is up to," George said and left the house.

"I need to talk with Mr. Will, the estate administrator, as mother suggested," George said out loud but out of earshot of William and Nancy, as if to declare to the world his future independence.

George Will was very receptive to talking to George about his future plans. George asked about his inheritance and Mr. Will said, "I won't know the exact amount until you near 21 years of age but I believe it will be over $200.00. That's a sizeable amount as I'm sure you know. Enough to support you for a number of years if you do decide to move off the farm and can't get work right away."

George was buoyed by that news and enthusiastically responded, "Some of my friends know people who have left this area and moved to larger cities. I know I can do the work these folks are doing — some working at a flour mill, some on lake boats moving iron ore and grain to the east, some working at grain storage areas loading and unloading the boats."

"What about college, George? You would probably have to work full time every other year to pay for it but what about that road? I graduated from college but my parents could afford to send me and paid for it."

George realized there was no money for college study since they'd nearly lost the farm a few years ago. He was prepared for the question and responded immediately.

"I can't do that — it would take me about eight years, since I'd have to earn the money as I went to pay for it, and my goal is to eventually buy a farm of my own. I don't need college training for farming. I don't know if I can save enough to ultimately buy a farm, but I need to try."

"George, if you're set on doing so, I do think you need to seek a good-paying job so you can add to your inheritance. I think it would probably take about a $1,000.00, a very large amount. It would probably take about four years or more, figuring your living expenses, of solid work and savings to convince a banker to loan a young single man enough to buy a farm."

Well, okay, thought George, and responded in a straightforward manner. "Do you know what job is best and where I can find work?"

"I like the way you're approaching this decision, George, and I'm flattered you would ask me for advice, but I'm sure you've talked with your parents as well. William Houston is a successful businessman and farmer and I know he will give you advice also," said Mr. Will.

He knew George at some point would have to break the news to his mother and stepfather that he would be leaving the farm.

George Will did not want to alienate the Hustons, who might think he had persuaded George to leave. As estate administrator, he wanted to keep on good terms, since the youngest child, Otto, wouldn't reach 21 for another 13 years.

"Tell you what I can do," said George Will. "I get to Bowling Green about twice a month and will inquire of some friends about various possibilities for a young man wanting to work and save for the future."

They shook hands, George thanked him for his time, and Mr. Will asked George to come back in about a month or so.

George was of course anxious to learn more and when a month went by, he returned to Mr. Will's office.

"Come in George. I've got some interesting news."

George had been thinking about moving and was unsure where to move to and what jobs to look for. He had considered the possibility of Cleveland or Detroit and had definite thoughts but kept them to himself as George Will began the discussion.

George, like his father, was very ambitious and not afraid to take a risk. He decided his best chance to find work was to move to a large town, but it was a toss-up with Detroit to the north or Cleveland to the east.

He chose Detroit. He had heard there was a large surrounding farming community, not unlike Cleveland, and he thought of Detroit as more exciting, with Canada just across the Detroit River and Detroit the only large city in southeastern Michigan. He rationalized that Detroit would have more job opportunities than Cleveland. He reasoned that Detroit, situated on a major river, had a large protected ship dockage area whereas Cleveland, being directly on a large lake, did not. Ships would need to change course in their eastern or western travel to reach

Cleveland whereas the Detroit docks were directly on their course.

He thought also that the man-made Cleveland harbor might have limited capacity whereas Detroit had miles of shoreline for docks. Also, he reasoned, the Ohio River at Cincinnati and the Maumee River port at Toledo were competition for Cleveland while Detroit stood alone in southeastern Michigan. Additionally, he had heard stories that the nightlife in Detroit, with Canada just across the river, was more varied than Cleveland's.

"I talked with some people in Bowling Green about your questions. Some are in banking, handling business loans, so they know where the money is going and consequently where the jobs are."

George was listening intently as Mr. Will continued.

"I had lunch with a friend of mine in Bowling Green, Judge Hill, who is active in the stock market and follows commerce, that is business matters, especially in the Midwestern states of Ohio, Indiana, and Michigan. He said the Detroit Board of Trade had put pressure on the prosperous Wabash Railroad to run a rail line from Butler, Indiana, direct to Detroit, right up to the grain elevators on the Detroit River. This would allow the Wabash to ship grain, especially corn, from Indiana and points west, direct to the elevators in Detroit, for lake shipment to Buffalo and points east, such as New York City. Cheaper than shipping all the way by rail."

Mr. Will continued, "Judge Hill said the current annual volume of corn at the Detroit elevators is about 400,000 bushels but when the tracks are completed, the volume is expected to reach 2 to 5 million bushels per year. This means that the grain business in Detroit will expand greatly once the line is completed in a year or so. So the future looks bright for workers in Detroit who handle grain shipments east by boat."

This was welcome news as George Will continued.

"I thanked Judge Hill and told him I would pass it on to an ambitious young man in Weston. He of course was familiar with your father's estate since he appointed me as administrator, and he was anxious to help."

"Now," continued George Will, "you expressed some interest in working on shipping vessels. There are many jobs on lake ships but there's a downside. Every year there are some ships lost in storms and some lives lost. And ships don't work in winter so the job would be seasonal."

"The railroads are hauling more and more grain from the farms and this is a growing business. As I mentioned, the Wabash Railroad Line will open the Midwest corn-belt to the Port of Detroit. Detroit is already a grain center but so is Toledo. Cleveland handles a little grain but not nearly as big as Toledo or Detroit. Chicago is even bigger but of course further away from Weston," said Mr. Will.

"So it sounds like Toledo or Detroit are my best bets," said young George.

"I think so, if you want to stay reasonably close to your family in Weston — say a day or two of travel," said the administrator.

"Now, I have even more information. There are storage facilities at these cities that require a lot of men to operate. They are loading grain into ships and train cars for shipment east. Most are shoveling grain and are called scoopers. They work all year long at the storage areas, which are referred to as elevators. Guess the name came about since the grain is elevated quite high up to allow loading the vessels or train cars by use of gravity. The process is mechanized so you won't have to carry bags or baskets of grain up eight floors for storage. There's a continuous vertical belt that scoops the grain at ground level and dumps it at the top. There are buckets attached to the moving belt, all powered by a steam engine."

"So George, that's my advice. I think you need to decide what city to move to and go to the elevators and ask for a job. I would think the elevator owners would be happy to have a hard-working farm boy join their crew. And I was told Detroit has about six elevators so that makes your chance of getting steady work even better."

Mr. George Will was smugly satisfied that he was able to get so much information to help his young charge, and George's guardian, William Martin, would be happy to learn of their conversation as well.

Obviously, George was very pleased. He left Mr. Will's office feeling encouraged and recognizing his logic about Detroit was correct. "Detroit it is!" George said aloud as he began the walk to the Houston's farms.

He did just that when he reached 21 and received his inheritance from the estate administrator, George W. Will, and his guardian, William Martin. It was a sizeable sum of $339.00 — well over a year's wages at a high-paying industrial job in the year 1888. It was a very good start for a young man striving to eventually buy a farm of his own. He banked the bulk of his fortune in Bowling Green but kept $50.00 to support striking out on his own. "This should tide me over until I find a steady paying job and settle into life in Detroit," he told his mother and father-in-law.

Right or wrong, with some inheritance money in his pocket, he was off to Detroit. His inheritance was a healthy start in saving for his goal and would more than tide him over until he found work. He was an optimistic, happy person who thought his chances of finding a job in Detroit would be pretty good. He recognized his inheritance was a great start toward his goal and he was not about to squander it, so he was intent on finding a job as soon as possible to pay for his room and board, some entertainment, and to save money for a future farm.

His farm work in Ohio plus an upbeat disposition proved helpful in getting a job at a grain elevator in Detroit. The elevator serviced the Detroit area gristmills with wheat and oats for making floor and corn for making corn meal. Of course, large quantities of grain were shipped from the elevators down the Detroit River into the connecting waterways to ports east.

One of his responsibilities was unloading incoming grain wagons from farms surrounding Detroit, including those around the village of Mt. Clemens. Thus he would interface with area farmers while unloading the wagons.

For farmers to convert their grain to money, they needed to transport their grain to a grist mill or grain elevator. They would be paid based on the equivalent bushels delivered or credited with the amount for payment at a later date. The Mallasts made many such trips following each year's harvests, turning the golden grain into cash. After many trips during the 1880s, they got to know the elevator workers pretty well. In 1889 they noticed a new hand at the job, a young man who had recently moved from a small village in north central Ohio. It was George Anthony they encountered.

August Mallast had agreed with son Adolph's plan to expand their acreage from 40 to 75. At the time, August thought they would have difficulty farming all 75 acres without help.

"Not to tell the boys — don't want to discourage them before we try. Maybe I'll be surprised but let's see how it goes for the first year," he spoke out loud while feeding their carriage horse, whom he now called Wolfgang out of longing for his old companion in Prussia.

The 1891 harvest was finally in with the last field of corn being husked by Emil and Fred. The whole family was near exhaustion, especially August and the boys. Even Rose and the girls pitched in doing lesser tasks such as poultry coop cleaning and feeding poultry and livestock and helping with the field harvest. Emil and Fred, still teenagers, were depended upon to carry an adult workload.

Emil and Fred had been looking forward to the less demanding time after the harvest season. Some time for hunting right after the corn was husked and some grain set aside for next year's planting along with feed for the pigs and poultry. They had just finished the seed wheat cleaning, separating more chaff from the wheat with the hand-powered fanning machine, when August came into the barn.

"Emil and Fred, you need to start your grain sale trips to Detroit while the roads are in good shape. You know the roads will be impassable if we get a wet fall, and as you know, the Michigan weather is bound to change as we get closer to winter," August said in his military command voice.

"All right," said Emil, "we'll start but tomorrow we were planning on doing some hunting since we've been working so hard. We'll try to bag a few of those pheasants and ducks that have been feeding in our corn fields. That's one good thing about losing some corn kernels during the shucking. I can taste those juicy pheasants now."

"Okay, Emil," August said. "One day for hunting and then getting the wagon ready the next day. Then off you two go to the grain elevator in the big city. Make the same contact at the Union Railroad Elevator because we want our grain to go to the higher-priced English market at Liverpool, even though it's a risky prospect. But," added August, "if we want to earn enough to buy a farm, we need to take the gamble. If not, 40 years from now you boys will still be renting and saying the same thing: 'Wish we had enough to buy a farm.'"

Emil and Fred were excited as they got the Remington side-by-side double barrel shotgun and shells ready to head out before dawn next morning. After getting their hunting pack ready, they set out for the cornfield to dig a one-man pit to hide in. Emil and Fred placed a few cornstalks over the hole and gathered a few ears of corn they found scattered about the field. They placed the corn and their six hand-carved decoys near the pit for setup next morning. They needed to gauge the wind direction next morning and set up downwind, scattering the corn and placing the decoys a short distance downwind from the pit. The ducks would come in from downwind, setting their wings and gliding into the wind for more lift. They would glide down toward the corn and the already "feeding ducks" — the decoys.

"That's how I hope it works," said Emil to Fred.

They woke up early next morning, responding to their internal clock, grabbed their pack and shotgun and walked briskly to the field. They placed the decoys and some corn about 20 feet away from the pit, with the brisk October wind at the shooter's back.

Emil explained to younger Fred, "There, when the ducks set their wings, they'll be in direct sight without needed to twist our necks to see them come in for a landing."

Then Emil took two twigs of different length, held them in his clenched fist, concealing their lengths, and told Fred, "Pick one — if it's the short one you can shoot first. The loser needs to run over to the lane fence and lay in the tall grass so the ducks won't see him, probably you, Fritz."

Fred picked and let out a hoot after seeing Emil had the long twig.

"I win, Emil! Won't be long before first light — I'll get in the pit and wait for the first flight in."

"Okay, lucky brother," said Emil, "but when you drop your first one, or when you have two flights in and miss, it's my turn. Don't pretend to forget 'cause I'll be running to the pit for my turn before the sun comes up and butterflies are the only thing in the sky. It's only late October, so these will probably be local mallards or maybe some teal or widgeon, since they start their migration early in the season."

Emil knew it wouldn't take very long for local ducks to get wise to being shot at and clear out for the day. "Looks like a clear day, so I hope I get a shot," he said to himself as he munched his breakfast, lying concealed in the tall grass by the rail fence.

Fred, in the pit, could see a small flock of four ducks flying over the woods in the gray light mist of morning. Looks like they were headed to the cornfield all right — they were probably here yesterday and want some more of their favorite golden food.

They were bigger than teal and the wing beat was slower, so they were probably the more tasty mallards.

"That's great," he thought. "Come on, ducks, look at the decoys."

Now they were flying directly toward the decoys, the corn, and the pit.

"That's it — they're setting their wings for a landing. Wait, wait, come closer," Fred excitedly told himself. "Now!"

He rapidly moved some cornstalks out of the way, took a bead on the lead duck, its wings spread and set for landing, and fired. He did not have to lead the duck since they were gliding into the wind, which was at his back. The lead duck was hit, wings folded, and plummeted to the ground. He then aimed the Remington double barrel at one of the rapidly retreating mallards who was now at an angle to him. This shot was more difficult since the ducks were rapidly flying away at an angle and he would need to accurately lead one of the startled mallards. He pulled the trigger, but this time the pellets whistled behind the rapidly retreating mallard as the ducks hurriedly flew to the lake and safety.

Emil had been watching and knew those ducks would not be back — once was enough for them.

"They're pretty smart," he said as he reached the pit while Fred was retrieving the evening meal. "That's going to be light eating for the entire family with only one duck to go around," he jokingly chided Fred, then added, "My turn. Quick, run to the fence while I get set up in the pit. Maybe we'll be lucky and another flock will come in for a breakfast of fresh corn kernels," he shouted as Fred ran to the fence.

Emil anxiously looked at the horizon but knew the blue sky meant their duck hunting was nearly over for the day. After an hour or so, a lone mallard flew in from Emil's back and surprised him. To his delight, the mallard turned and circled the decoys, not too sure of landing but surely interested. Yes — he was setting his wings.

"Now we'll have a good supper with enough of the tasty mallards to go around," Emil thought. He waited as the mallard's wings played on the stiff lake breeze, gliding in toward the pit. At the last minute, the duck, with its excellent eyesight, must have see Emil, for it started beating his wings frantically to get out of there fast. But it was too late — Emil led the duck perfectly and made a good shot. His heart was beating rapidly as he saw the wings fold and watched the downed mallard hit the ground.

Fred came racing out from the lane fence and told Emil, "Good shot, brother. Now we've got enough for a good meal. You know, this is better than hiding in the cornstalk teepee, cause it's so much easier to see the ducks come and get in shooting position."

"You're right, Fred, but the teepee really hides you well. That duck spotted me as he was coming in. I think with a big flight of 20 or so, both methods are very effective."

Fred got in the pit to take another turn, but Emil knew this butterfly day wouldn't offer good hunting. He was thinking maybe they could take Duke out after an early afternoon milking session and rustle up a pheasant or two.

After about an hour with no more flying, Emil walked toward the pit.

"Let's go in, Fred — there won't be any action now. The sun has been up for a couple hours and the breeze is dying down.

We have the Detroit trip to get ready for and I would like to pheasant hunt after this afternoon's milking."

Fred, hoping to get another few shots in before the fun ended, reluctantly agreed.

"All right, big brother. I look forward to a night in Detroit — that will be a welcome change and as usual another adventure."

Emil agreed and reminded Fred, "Maybe we'll see that guy we met last year, the Anthony guy from Ohio. Hope he's still working at our elevator. Be good to know someone friendly who can fill us in on places to go and where not to go."

Fred mischievously replied, "Maybe the places not to go are the places we should go."

"You're much too young, little brother. Just listen to your worldly older brother — I'll take care of you," said Emil.

The boys put the decoys in a burlap bag and headed for the house. They carried their two mallards, hoping their mother would volunteer to clean the ducks while they got the wagon ready to load grain early tomorrow morning.

Rose would have nothing to do with that, but the boys could tell, as they cleaned the ducks, that their mother and father were happy they'd brought home some tasty corn-fed mallards for dinner this evening.

Fred, toward evening, added to the fare. He'd won the twig test again and was given the first shot. Fred did bag a pheasant after running frantically behind their dog Duke, who was running full out, nose to the ground, following a rooster scent from the corn field to the pasture.

Next morning, Emil and Fred arose earlier than usual, pleased with their previous day's hunting and excited about the trip. They needed to take the first load of the season to the Union Railroad Company Elevator in Detroit as commanded by their father. They woke their father before heading toward the barn to hitch up the two workhorses.

"You guys will have a long walk today," Fred said to the two big workhorses in the horse stalls. He put the bit, collar, and reins on each and walked them to the wagon. They hitched the horses to the draw bar and led the team and wagon into the barn, next to the granary. By this time August had made a pot of coffee on the kitchen wood stove and brought them each a large mug, knowing they had a full day ahead of them. Emil and Fred had greased the axles and looked over the wagon bed carefully the day before, to assure there were no gaps in the bed. This was important since they did not want any of their hard-earned, precious wheat cargo to escape.

The boys stopped to gulp down their coffee before grabbing their scoop shovels and going to work. They knew the two horses could pull about 25 bushels and had marked the inside of the box bed to indicate when they had reached that amount, which was about three-quarters of a ton or 1500 pounds.

Rose had packed them a lunch and after a big breakfast, they gave the horses a good long drink of water and started down the Lake Road to Detroit, some 20 miles away. It was seven o'clock by this time. Emil said to younger Fred, "The trip should take about eight hours, so we should arrive at the elevator around three o'clock. I hope our guy George, who we worked with last year, is still working at the unloading platform."

Fred responded, "Same here, Emil, he was fun to work with. Good sense of humor and nearly as hard a worker as me."

"Boy, that doesn't say very much. I think our youngest sister can work harder than you, Fritz," Emil said to goad Fred on.

"Humph, just for that you can drive all the way. I'm going to lie down on the canvas-covered wheat and take a long nap!" Fred responded while crawling into the back of the wagon to lie down with his straw hat pulled over his face.

The trip was uneventful and they arrived in line at the elevator right around four o'clock. Emil had a chance to nap as well, since Fred forgave his brother and took over driving near the foot of the Eight Mile Road.

They were happy to see George Anthony working on the platform, helping to shovel grain into the holding pit and operating the scoop belt lift. They made their presence known and when the two wagons ahead of them were unloaded, they drove their wagon up the ramp onto the unloading platform. A wagon scale was used to weigh the loaded wagon, then the empty weight was obtained.

The boys chatted away with George who was typically in good spirits. Emil suggested they meet for dinner after checking into the hotel and seeing to the horses at the hotel livery. George, always looking for something different to do, was very receptive and they made plans to meet at his boarding house and have supper together. But before leaving, Emil made sure their weight was recorded with the grain dealer, Dan Steward, so that the Mallast account was credited with today's weight, and slated for sale in Liverpool. Emil received a receipt from Dan and tucked it in his money pouch, securely tied around his midsection, under his shirt.

It was now late afternoon and George needed to finish unloading another wagon. They agreed to meet at seven o'clock at George's boarding house.

George told them, "It's about a mile from the river, down Gratiot Street, then go left on Riopelle Street. There is a sign in front, 'Carmen Cashing and Joseph Reno Boarding House' in the front of the building. Just go in and ask for me. I eat supper there but tonight I'll take a night out with Emil and Fred Mulke."

Both boys at once said, "No, no George — it's Mallast — Mallast!"

"Okay, I'll try to remember. It's a French name, isn't it?" he asked in dry humor fashion, knowing they were German by their lingering European accents.

The horses responded to the light-weight, empty wagon with a brisk walking pace as Emil drove the wagon to the Eisenbord House at the corner of Cass and Lewis Streets.

Emil told Fred, "The Eisenbord House is kind of expensive, $1.00 to $2.00 a day but that includes the livery service. They advertise the Eisenbord as having the best and most convenient barn in the city for farmers' teams. The horses will be glad to get a good long drink and some fresh hay."

They arrived at the Cashing-Reno boarding house closer to eight o'clock than seven. George was waiting in the downstairs setting room and introduced them to one of the three current owners, Theresa Bark.

"Why do you stay at the Eisenbord? You must be rich," said Theresa.

"They have a stable for the horses," said Emil.

"We can fix that — we'll tie them in the back and let them eat the wild grass. And we can give them leftover vegetables as well. Next time, stay with us, that is, if we have an open room."

Emil was noncommittal, sensing correctly that she was kidding with them.

She continued, "Our house may be changing soon — a Mr. Cairbo of southern Italy is negotiating to buy it. He's an ice dealer in Italy and wants to move to the United States. He's even picked out a name and plans on changing it to a saloon and restaurant. He plans to call it the Roma Café — I think because he said he wants to sail on the passenger ship called the *Roma*. Isn't that interesting to you! I'll bet our little talk will be the highlight of your journey to Detroit."

"Fascinating!" said Emil, who was playing along with George's boarding house owner.

"Now don't stay out late, boys — George has to work tomorrow, and more importantly, I don't want him getting sick and disturbing the sleeping roomers. You be careful, George — these guys may get you into trouble," Theresa said jokingly.

"Come with us, Theresa. You'll have a good time as well!" said Emil, giving tit for tat.

Theresa of course declined and off they went.

"I'm going to take you to a German restaurant called Schweitzers," said George. "It's near the river so it's not far away. And you'll feel right at home because you can even order in German if you like. But probably they won't understand you because your accent has been receding into a real American one. But you can try anyway. They have very good food. Oh, you do understand it's Dutch treat, don't you? You may not have heard that term before — it means we each pay for our own dinner."

Emil and Fred were now worried that the restaurant might be too expensive for them.

"We only have three dollars left after paying for the hotel and horse barn," said Emil.

"That should work and even leave enough for a good Goebel Pilsner beer. I wonder if that's a French beer?" said George jokingly.

Fred spoke up and in a very serious tone and said, "Sounds German to me."

The dinner was good but left Emil and Fred with only about a dollar left.

"What are we going to tell Father?" said Fred with genuine concern. "We usually bring back about two dollars."

George felt Fred's panic.

"Tell you what, Fred. I'll lend you and Emil a dollar or two for a couple glasses of beer. That is, if you promise to pay me back when you bring your next load of wheat to the elevator. That way, you guys won't be thrown into the dungeon when you get back to your farm. What do you say? Does that make you both feel better?"

"Sounds great. Let's shake on it," said Emil.

"Oh no!" said George. "I need you to sign in blood. Here, I have a pocketknife."

They all broke out in laughter.

"Okay, that's settled, we'll shake, and now we're off to the Eschenbach Saloon, very near the river on Atwater Street. Next time you come to the elevator, I'll take you to the Deulsches Haus saloon. You can repay your loan there."

They had a good time, and even Fred was able to share some of Emil's beverage — Emil, pretending to be the dutiful brother, jokingly told Fritz he wasn't old enough to drink a full stein. By the time they drove into the farmyard next evening, they were really ready for bed, but first they needed to bed, water, and feed the horses and milk the cows. They ate a good dinner, dragged themselves upstairs, pulled their work clothes off, and collapsed on their beds. They started sawing logs so loud that August hollered up, "Snore more quietly!"

They returned in two weeks with a second load. This time, they met George for supper at their hotel. They ate in the hotel dining room so it wasn't as expensive as the Schweitzers but George insisted they then go to the Rimy Bourgeois saloon near the river on St. Aubin Street instead of the Deulsches Haus.

"Even though they have expensive French wine, they also have a pale lager beer that is quite good and bottled locally by the Koppitz-Melcher Brewing Co. It's the brewer's specialty. In fact, it's called pale select lager," George said with emphasis on "select."

They were seated and ordered a round of the pale lager. Fred lucked out and was given a glass. Even though he hadn't developed a taste for beer, he had to pretend for fear of being razed by George and Emil.

"My friends," George spoke, "this might be our last meeting."

Both Emil and Fred were aghast.

"What do you mean, George?" Emil said.

"I am intrigued by the ships sailing from here to Buffalo and other ports," said George. "It looks like a good life and the crew members seem friendly enough. I've become friends with some crewmembers on a schooner, that's a sailing ship, usually with two masts but there are some three-mast schooners. These are the larger ones of course. Anyway, *Daniel G. Fort* is the schooner's name and it left Detroit yesterday, headed to Lake Ontario and the Port of Oswego, in New York state," George replied.

He continued, "You'd be interested, the *Daniel G. Fort* is carrying the Mallast grain as part of its load of 11,000 bushels of wheat to New York City. I'm told the canal route from Oswego is shorter than the route from Buffalo to New York. Oswego is a more direct water route but ships have to go through a series of locks at the Welland Canal, to lower them from the higher waters of Lake Erie to Lake Ontario, and this bypasses a huge waterfall. So I'm thinking about the glamorous life on the lakes. I would miss seeing you both but that's what I'm thinking about when I say it may be the last time we have a meal and a beer together."

Emil and Fred were both saddened by the news but wished him well if he did decide to join the *Daniel G. Fort's* crew. The boys took a closer interest in the ships dockside as they passed the Michigan Central elevators. There was the *Albert L. Andrews*, the *Blue Star*, and the *Senator*. All were schooners being loaded or waiting their turn to receive the long boon-like tube from the waterside loading tower, filled with cascading golden grain plunging into the bowels of the vessels.

"Too bad, Fred," said Emil. "I think we'll both miss George if he does decide to ship out."

"Yes," said Fred, as the sun climbed off the horizon. "He is a good guy with a sense of humor and a hard worker."

The next trip to the Union Railroad Elevator was the following week. They needed to make regular trips to deliver their increased acreage harvest of 600 bushels of wheat and 150 bushels of corn. They were happily surprised to find George working as usual on the unloading deck!

"George, so good to see you," both Emil and Fred said nearly in unison.

"Did you change your mind or hasn't the *D. G. Fort* returned from Lake Ontario yet?" Emil asked.

"It's not going to return," said George. "There was a north-east gale blowing for two or three days. Wind right down the long lake, waves building to eight feet, I'm told. A really bad storm, but I'm told not unusual during the fall shipping season on the Great Lakes. The *Daniel G. Fort* has been sunk and the crew was in real danger. A tug towing the ship into the safety of the harbor got out of sync with the wave action and the towline broke. The *D. G. Fort* was a sailing ship and didn't have propeller power. It was at the mercy of the wind and waves and was dashed onto the outer shoal.

"The crew had to be terrified, looking death in the face," George continued. "They might have drowned except, fortunately for them, the United States lifesaving crew at the port had anticipated a possible wreck because of the fierce northeast gale. They were able to shoot a line over the vessel and the crew members, one by one, were pulled from the sinking ship to shore in a sort of closed can called a breeches' buoy. It had to be really scary. Anyway, the glorious lake life doesn't seem so glorious now."

"And the *D. G. Fort* wasn't the only sinking at Oswego," George added. "A schooner named the *Wayne* was dashed to bits on the rocks a year earlier and the *Baltic* was lost just three days before the *D. G. Fort* went on the shoal.

"I've decided to stick to the land life," George concluded. "Also, there would have to be long stretches of routine boat life sailing from port to port. No nightlife in the middle of a lake.

So you're stuck with seeing me during your wagon trips to the big city and drinking a few bottles of good French beer," George said jokingly.

"German beer, George!" they both responded.

"Fantastic news!" said Emil.

"That's great!" said Fred.

As usual, they had a good time, especially celebrating George's news. The saloon was a type of rathskeller, with lots of singing and crowd participation, so it was a very exciting and fun night for the rural farm boys. They had a good time!

They set off for home the next morning, talking to each other and saying they couldn't wait until the next trip. Emil and Fred described some but not all of their adventures to the family following each trip.

As their father had thought from the start, the brothers recognized the need for more help on the 1890 expanded farm, which increased actual crop acreage from 27 to 62. They all recognized firsthand what doubling their grain acreage meant in terms of their increased work. Although the plan was a sound and even necessary one to reach their goal of buying the farm, the increased workload was initially underappreciated. So it was in 1891 that the brothers, Emil and Fred, knowing firsthand the result of Adolph's plan in renting substantially more acreage, knew the family needed another farmhand.

"Why hasn't Father recognized this?" Emil said to Fred.

"Maybe he wants to work us all the time, even on Sundays," Fred responded.

"We have to convince Father that we need to hire someone to help — it's not fair that we need to work from morning to night, all the time. We need some time to ourselves," Emil continued.

"Wouldn't it be great if we could convince father to hire help and convince George to work on our farm? We need a farmhand badly, so why not George?"

They decided it would be great if their newfound grain elevator friend would move to the farm and work with them. They really liked their new friend, George Anthony from Ohio, so in their eyes it was a win-win situation, if they could pull it off. George would get a different farm experience and a quasi-second family to boot, while the boys would get badly needed help on the farm.

They had decided to give it a go, but knew it would be a formidable task. First, they needed to convince George that it was an opportunity he should not pass up. Second, they needed to convince their father that it was a necessary step for the farm to prosper.

They worked on George first. After a few trips and a couple more nights in Detroit with George as their guide, they lobbied that working on their farm was a great idea. It would be hard work for six days, but it would be mostly outdoors in the fresh air and sunshine near a beautiful lake. He would take his meals with the family and they could party together every Saturday night with the family and neighbors on the farm or occasionally in the wild village of Mt. Clemens.

George wasn't so sure. Being a sociable young single male, he liked the hustle and bustle of city life. He enjoyed the bachelor life in Detroit and an occasional night across the Detroit River in Canada. But all was not fun and games. There were lonesome times as well and he did miss his family. So a family environment appealed to him. He would live at the farm and take meals with the family. He did like Emil and Fred, based on their Detroit trips and socializing with them. And he perceived, based on the boys' descriptions, the Mallast family to be a friendly, caring group. In fact the family, as portrayed by the boys, reminded him of his own family in Ohio. He imagined the Mallast girls to be like his older sister, Della, who always seemed to keep things in a state of flux.

George continued to think as they chatted away over dinner at the Saloon. He did have a steady job, although it lacked the variety a farm life provided. And his goal was to own his own farm one day, so the experience would be good, especially comparing the flat land of the Ohio farm to a lakeside farm located on a river delta. He would save on room and board, which the boys said would be furnished, but probably make much less money.

"It sounds intriguing," he told Emil and Fred. "Let me think about it and I'll let you know on your next grain trip."

They clicked their tankards to cement the promise, even Fritz, who by now they considered nearly an adult.

"Now for step two," Emil said to his younger brother Fred on the trip home. "We have to convince Father to hire him."

They gathered their courage after a big Sunday dinner and asked their father to listen to their proposal.

August did not let on but was very amused when Emil hesitantly proposed hiring help. To the boys' surprise, it turned out to be a soft sell since August, keeping his thoughts to himself so as not to discourage the boys, had recognized early on the need for more help.

Adolph had also thought they might need additional help when he'd proposed the acreage expansion to his father, but he hadn't brought it up, afraid of dampening their enthusiasm for expanded acreage, especially since Emil and Fred would not be developed to full strength for a number of years. So after the first year of backbreaking harvest work in farming the much larger acreage, all the Mallasts recognized the need.

August was especially interested when the boys said they had just the person in mind. He listened to his sons' high recommendations and their urging to hire the grain elevator man from Ohio. They attested he was a good worker at the elevator and therefore should be a good worker on the farm and had farm experience in Ohio. Further, Fred and Emil stated, he was friendly and of good character.

August trusted his sons' opinion and agreed to take him on, and the boys were delighted. They couldn't wait for the next grain trip so they could tell George the family wanted him to join them in working the lakeside farm.

August pondered how much to pay the hired hand. He told Emil to offer room, board, and $2.00 per week and point out to George that he did not have to pay room rent or for Rose's delicious cooking.

August decided a hired man would not live in the house and told the boys they would need to build a room in the southwest corner of the barn. Although it was more work for them, they happily agreed and were delighted. They began work on the room after a trip to the village for wood boards and a potbelly stove plus nails and stove pipes. They couldn't wait for their next trip to the elevator to tell George the good news.

The trip occurred two weeks later. They returned with another load of grain and again urged the Ohioan, George Anthony, to work with them on their lakeside farm.

George was told the pay was $2.00 per week but included room and board and that they had built a room for him. And they pointed out that their mother's cooking was superb and further, that George could put aside his entire week's pay if he wanted. He could save it all for a down payment on a farm since he wouldn't have other expenses except miscellaneous items.

George was thinking as the boys were talking. If he took the job, he would not only get a change from the grain elevator routine but he'd be working with new friends in a family setting. Further, he reasoned, he would be gaining more farm experience from a different perspective, i.e., Michigan farming on delta rich soil versus Ohio plains without a lot of water. He would be able to save for his dream without contending with spending temptations he frequently encountered in Detroit. He would also be part of an upbeat family that did not have a lot of past tragedy to contend with. Also, he would be able to associate with the girls on the farm, Emil and Fred's sisters he'd heard so much about.

George told the boys he would accept their offer and asked them to delay their return a few hours next day until he could settle accounts, pack his few belongings, and ride to the farm with them. The boys were elated!

George was not disappointed in the Mallast family or the farm. Both girls were full of fun, having grown to young maturity in the rural setting along the shores of Lake St. Clair with its clear water and sandy bottom. Emilie was full of energy, always running, whereas Bertha was more subdued and very pretty.

The lake was a big selling point for Emil and Fred, and they anticipated great fun on hot summer evenings following nightly chores with their new hired hand. On their drive to the Mallast farm along the Lake Road, the jubilant salesmen continued to encourage and reassure George. They informed him that the water was clean and clear with northern offshore winds.

Southern winds would kick up the sand as the waves neared shore, making the water appear cloudy, but in reality this was only clean sand, suspended in the turbulent water. An onshore wind, they said, wasn't very typical since the prevailing winds were from the west.

"The lake frontage water will be excellent for swimming and bathing following a hard day of farm chores, even with a south wind," Fred told George.

"The south wind does have a very favorable aspect — the breeze reaches the farmhouse, carrying with it the very pleasant lake aroma of sun, wind, and water," Emil explained. He added, "The sandy, shallow bottom at the shoreline is excellent for swimming and just plain having fun like playing catch and splashing water at our sisters."

The family bathed in the lake in summer and early fall, using soap made from animal fat saved from the kitchen cooking. But with the arrival of George on the farm, the girls needed to be especially careful in scheduling their baths at a suitable time. Brothers were one thing, but a new, young, handsome hired man stumbling onto their bathing would be a very embarrassing experience. At least to the girls!

The Mallasts had acquired a small 16-foot rowboat that allowed George and the brothers, Fred and Emil, to fish and swim in deeper waters offshore. Lake perch, a delicious fish, were very plentiful along with walleye and an occasional lake bass or the vicious pike. These provided a nice variety for the Mallast table.

With George hired, Sundays would again be days of rest, both boys thought. They did have more leisure time, and Fred and Emil often took George on the rowboat, trying their luck at fishing and taking frequent swimming breaks to cool off.

This was a new experience for the young man who hailed from land-locked Ohio.

George enjoyed these outdoors activities a great deal. He learned how to trap muskrats in the winter and how to shoot the family's Remington double barrel shotgun while duck hunting. He grew to relish the summer and fall seasons during his years at the Mallast farm. Winters, however, were a different story.

Despite being happy on the Mallast farm, George felt a slight longing for his homestead in Ohio and wrote to his mother and stepfather every other week or so. The letters were usually mailed by Rose during the family's supply trips to Mount Clemens.

George was given a room that the Mallasts prepared in the front of the barn, complete with a potbelly woodstove standing on a stone base, the stovepipe carefully insulated against contact with the inside and outside walls of the room and barn. He had a bed, lantern, small table, and chair — what more could a young man require? He was fat, dumb, and happy, so to speak, in his 16 by 16 foot room.

George took his meals with the family and was allowed the use of the family's portable clothes washer and winter bathing tub. He soon got to be comfortable with the Mallast family, and they with him.

CHAPTER TEN

Bertha Mallast

LOVE AND OHIO

George Anthony was 24 when he joined the Mallast farm in the fall of 1891. As Emil and Fred drove the wagon into the farmyard, the nearby family members dropped their chores and came to welcome him. He was well within the age group of the Mallast children, since Rudolph was 29 and Bertha 14.

The girls were anxious to meet the young man they'd heard so much about from their brothers. They looked forward to having a single young man in their midst, creating a new dimension to their rather isolated farm.

"This will make our weekend nights with the neighbors more exciting," Emilie said to Bertha. "Now our neighbors, Billy Moore and the Villerot boys, Lucien and Ernest, will have some dancing competition when we have our Saturday night dancing."

August and Adolph were in the fields, but at supper that evening they too expressed how happy they were that George was joining them and really looked forward to having his help. In the ensuing conversations, August was his usual reserved self, preferring to observe the family dynamics for a few weeks and wondering if his sons had exaggerated their description of George's work ethic. "Time will tell," he told Rose as they prepared for bed later that evening.

The farm had been expanded from 40 acres to 110 acres thanks in large part to Adolph who initiated the discussion of increasing acreage. Even though 35 acres were marshland and not farmable, the remaining acres nearly doubled the farm size, making the entire acreage unmanageable without hired help. George took on his responsibility and pulled his weight as the hired hand. As time went on, the entire family, even August, grew to like George.

George was especially liked by Bertha, who at 14 was starting to take a keen interest in boys. Emilie was also taken with George, but he seemed most comfortable with Bertha, even though she was 10 years his junior. Emilie, at 23, was only one year his junior and George found her more difficult to deal with. Plus, George thought Bertha was very good-looking and had recognized she had a quiet demeanor, so the two got along very well right from the start. They both loved the farm life, the lake, the family, and rural living.

Bertha liked George's fun-loving attitude, his energy, and his self-confidence. She learned George had seen many tragedies in his family and that he appreciated the cohesiveness and upbeat character of the Mallasts.

George often wrote his mother and stepfather about the farm, the Mallasts, and especially Bertha, so much so that his mother, Nancy Ann, and stepfather, William Houston, felt they knew her. They knew George liked farming, and Nancy knew he was like his father, both a risk taker and very ambitious.

"He will own a farm of his own someday," Nancy said to her second husband, William Houston.

William, knowing Nancy missed her son, floated an idea.

"We own a substantial amount of farm property; why not offer George a parcel? Not give it to him, but sell it to him, so he has a chance to work for it and feel the accomplishment of doing so?"

Although Nancy couldn't read or write, her significant lifetime challenges had left her a wise person, and she jumped at his suggestion.

"I like it, William," she said. "He could realize his goal at a young age since he's only 26, and we would gain a son back to the homestead. He's been out on his own for five years now so maybe he would consider returning."

The very next day, with the help of her studious fourteen-year-old son Otto, Nancy dictated a letter to George. With Otto doing the writing, she presented the opportunity to George.

George did want to branch out on his own as soon as possible, and he realized his mother's suggestion deserved his careful thought and a response fairly soon. He liked the Mallasts and the set up with the nearby lake and marsh and especially the beautiful Bertha, but this might be an opportunity too good to pass up. He would ask for time off during the coming Christmas season and visit his family on their Weston County farm in Ohio, but he wouldn't yet disclose the farm purchase possibility to the Mallasts. He wanted to learn more particulars before making a decision and he had to come to grips with his feelings about Bertha, now 16.

"I've know her for two years now, and I really like her," he said to Duke, the farm dog, as he continued swinging the scythe into the standing corn stalks that cloudy autumn day in 1893. Bertha was certainly a factor in his reasoning.

His mother listened as Otto read George's scrawling response.

"Wonder what grade he got in penmanship?" Otto asked his mother. Still, he could figure out most of George's script, enough to convey to his mother that George would visit during the holidays.

Now, what farmland should they offer him, and how much land, and what price should they set to make it a challenge?

William thought a 37-acre parcel, complete with farmhouse, in the adjoining section would be suitable. They knew George had the inheritance of about $350.00 or so and that he had been working for a full four years, it now being 1893.

"Not too much acreage so he can manage it fairly well, maybe needing hired help at times, and still have some time for himself," he told his wife. "We'll let him assume the $1,200.00 mortgage I gave the Union Central Life Insurance Company in Bowling Green. We should also ask for a sizeable down payment to challenge his personal savings strategy," William said. "How about $600.00?"

As planned, George did visit during the Christmas holidays and spent time with siblings and friends in the Weston area. He also looked over the property. He wanted to accept the offer, but he needed time to sort out his feelings about his life in Michigan. He had fallen in love with Bertha, now 17, and he believed she loved him. And he felt a real closeness to the Mallast family, especially a close brother-like relationship with Emil.

Nonetheless, he knew this was an opportunity to accomplish his farm ownership goal, and having gone through some tragic times, he was also anxious to create a happy life with Bertha. That is, if she would marry him, he thought to himself.

"These opportunities don't come along often," he said to his younger brother Otto as they returned home after looking at the property. He put the gelding into a gallop and the sleigh flew over the snow-covered road.

George did have $600.00 and a bit more saved. The remote farm life had allowed him to save nearly $200.00 at $2.00 per week, and two full years at the Union Railroad Elevator had allowed him to save about the same amount at a higher wage but with substantial living expenses of room, board, and entertainment in the exciting city of Detroit. This put his savings at about $400.00 but when including the inheritance, he was well over the $600.00 threshold. Buying his own farm was an opportunity he longed for. He was torn between achieving his goal and leaving the Mallast family and their lakeside farm.

Just before the new year began, George signed a purchase agreement and a promissory note to buy the farm in Ohio.

"We'll work out a formal mortgage agreement," William Houston told George as he accepted his note. A formal agreement was drawn up and George signed the document in January, 1894. His dream to own a farm was a reality, but he was not quite ready to break ties with the Mallasts.

He decided to spend another year at the Mallast farm, saving more money and learning more about farming, and possibly declaring his feelings for Bertha.

George's relationship with Bertha had elevated to a higher, more intimate level the previous summer. They'd enjoyed time alone, when they could evade Emil and Fred. Rowing the Mallast boat out into the lake, swimming during hot summer afternoons, and long walks strolling through the farm fields or on the Lake Road were some of their favorite pastimes. Their mutual interests had carried over with careful candor into the following year. As with many compatible young couples attracted to each other, the love bug was busily at work. The two spent hours together, discussing the future, and when George spoke with confidence about owning his own farm, Bertha was impressed. She was not aware that George had already signed a purchase agreement during his holiday visit to Ohio the previous winter.

As 1894 progressed, George was thinking about his return to Ohio, even though the planting and harvest seasons were a very busy time on the farm. Getting the field crops in plus the daily milk chores and caring for the livestock and poultry kept him very busy so he didn't have too much time to fret about the move, which had been relegated somewhat to the back of his mind.

It was a delightful summer, shared with Bertha and the family, which all too soon gave way to fall and then to winter. It was late fall when George decided to tell Bertha of the Ohio farm. He pledged Bertha to secrecy, then told her in quiet tones that he had bought a farm in Ohio. He explained it was near his family and they had offered to sell him a farm and had given him this opportunity. He told Bertha, "This is something that doesn't happen often and I couldn't pass it up. This will allow me to accomplish my goal of owning and working my own farm. Something I've wanted to do my whole life."

Bertha was of course very sad since she realized George would be leaving them and returning to Ohio. Wiping the tears away, she told George she would keep his secret but sobbing, she said, "George, I don't want you to leave!"

This was a difficult spot for the young man. He had anticipated this situation and had given it considerable thought, and he had a plan. He decided to ask Bertha to marry him on the spot, but he knew he needed to orchestrate this carefully. She might accept, but her parents might prevail and not allow the union. After all, Bertha was both the baby of the family at 17 and was very close to her family and, besides, he was only the hired man.

Bertha continued her crying and sobbing while George put his arm around her, comforting her. He asked, "Bertha, you know I love you. Will you marry me and come with me to Ohio?"

Bertha went limp in his arms as she responded, "Oh, yes, George, yes!"

While they planned how to break the news to her parents, somehow, during one of their romantic moments, Bertha became pregnant.

She broke the news to George in late winter. Now the couple really had a lot to talk about, and with a sense of urgency. What to do?

What to do was clear to George, but how to break the news to her parents?

"So much for my carefully worked out strategy," George said to himself. Happily, he'd asked Bertha to marry him months ago during the summer. Since he'd told her he'd bought a farm in Ohio, he'd convinced her that living there would be the best move for them. But he wasn't sure her parents would agree. Not only marrying their youngest daughter but taking her away from them, all the way to Ohio, would be hard for Bertha's parents to swallow. Clearly the Mallast farm now supporting two families, August's and Adolph's, could not provide enough income to also support the additional large family he hoped to have with Bertha.

The courtship had been very discreet and was initially unknown to Bertha's parents, though in plain sight of George's good buddies, Fred and Emil. They liked George and, of course, they thought their young sister was a thoughtfully good match to be his girlfriend. Hard to keep such things secret for long, and before they knew it, Rose realized that their baby was head over heels in love with George but she was not really prepared for the upcoming news.

George and Bertha wanted to marry as soon as possible, but Bertha was emphatic that they obtain her parents' consent and blessing first. George recognized they would need to break the news very carefully, especially since George was only the hired farmhand and Bertha was their baby girl.

It would be a big surprise and maybe even a shock to August and Rose.

George and Bertha decided the best time to break the news was after a Sunday dinner. Sunday dinners were always a special occasion on the farm, usually consisting of roast chicken and dumplings, potatoes, fresh or canned vegetables, and cake or pie. Following dinner, thanks to the extra help from George, the family could and usually did enjoy some leisure time playing games, reading, or engaging in some outdoor activity. George and Bertha thought this "feeling good time" was the best time to ask the question. Neither were at all certain how her parents would react.

George asked the question, but he was a bit nervous. After all, he needed to be certain that August and Rose understood what he said, since their English skills were still somewhat limited.

German was the main household language, although the children were picking up English, especially the boys, who had more opportunity to associate with others in conducting farm business.

August and Rose understood after George made the request with hand gestures, hugged Bertha, and repeated in a very few basic words, "Marry, love, together — okay?"

Their reaction was guarded. After all, George was 10 years older than Bertha, and she was only 17 years old. Rose was not prepared but at the same time wasn't too surprised since she was not oblivious to the romance. She was closer to Bertha, and she knew Bertha and George were more than good friends. Aided by this insight, she carefully explained to August, in German, what George had asked.

There was no doubt in August's mind now, and he was taken aback. Gathering his composure, he asked the frequently heard question by the father of a prospective bridegroom.

"How will you support Bertha? What will you do? Where will you live?"

George decided not to disclose his Ohio farm at this time. He thought it would be too much for Bertha's parents to accept. Marrying George and leaving Michigan also could result in her parents being adamantly opposed to the union. That would be some pickle, thought George to himself.

Rose liked George a great deal and pushed the request with August.

After much discussion in German, not understood by George, the prospective bridegroom started to worry. Besides the hired hand aspect, they might think of other reservations.

Finally, August gave way and extended George his hand, albeit rather reluctantly.

Bertha was happy beyond belief and hugged both her mother and father.

After the parents agreed, the very nervous George and Bertha broke the other news to August and Rose — that Bertha was expecting.

August was disappointed but kept his composure. His immediate thoughts centered on what a mistake it had been to take George on as a farmhand. This was followed by low-level anger.

Rose took another approach and lovingly put her arm around Bertha to comfort her. She spoke to August in German and calmed him down, convincing him to support the union. August finally concurred and embraced the couple.

This was February. It was decided the wedding should be as soon as possible in the spring.

They would need to schedule a date soon with the German Evangelical Protestant Church in Mount Clemens. The Mallasts didn't attend church every Sunday because of the remote location, but the pastor, Reverend Hermann Gundert, had come to know the family fairly well over the years. He was delighted to perform the ceremony. The Woltmans were invited along with some of the neighboring farm families along the Lake Road, the Villerots, Moores, and VandenBossches. George asked Emil to be his best man and Bertha asked Emilie to be the maid of honor.

George wrote a letter to his mother and stepfather but did not urge them to attend because of the long distance and expense.

The April, 1895, wedding day arrived with sunny and warm weather. The family left the farm early in the morning and traveled together by horse team and wagon, covering the five-mile trip to town in about two hours.

Rose had altered one of Bertha's best dresses to resemble a bridal gown of basic taste. The dress fit, albeit a bit snugly now that she was about four months along. Rose had purchased some material and made a long veil along with a sash that helped with the transformation. Bertha would freshen up and change at the church, so as to keep the dress fresh. Emilie helped with her hair and dress. George polished his shoes and wore his best shirt and trousers.

The church was a warm setting with sunlight streaming through the stained glass windows. The church pianist played a few hymns Bertha and George had selected while one of the church choir members sang two solos, both in German so the parents could better appreciate the holy union. Vows were also in German, but Bertha, who was somewhat fluent in the English language, with Pastor Gundert's concurrence, translated in a low voice for George. The Woltmans brought a bouquet of flowers, freshly picked from their yard. The entire Mallast family, the Woltmans, and a few farm neighbors filled the front pews of the small sanctuary nicely. The pianist played a wedding entrance march and a spirited piece at the conclusion. The couple was united in marriage. They signed the wedding document along with Pastor Gundert while Emil and Emilie signed as witnesses.

George's mother had written with their wish for happiness, and per George's suggestion, they did not attend because of the distance.

So it was with much joyful relief to Bertha and George that they were wed and with their parents' blessing. Bertha was extremely happy but somewhat apprehensive about their future. She did not know George's mother and she faced motherhood in the very near future.

The honeymoon was a night and day at the Avery House, one of Mount Clemens' finest hotels — at an exorbitant cost of $4 per night. After the short but romantic time at the hotel, George and Bertha returned to the Mallast farm. Brother Fred picked them up at the hotel late in the afternoon the day after the wedding, bringing the small buggy and his favorite horse, their second gelding, Danpatch, for the trip back to the farm.

Bertha moved into George's room at the farm, located at the southwest corner of the barn, and their married life began. They continued taking their meals at the house, with Bertha pitching in to help her sister and her mother to prepare the meals and help with household work. After a few weeks, she and George found the confines of the hired hand's 16 by 16 foot room getting smaller with each passing day.

The newlyweds discussed their situation and decided they wanted to strike out on their own sooner rather than later. George's farm was waiting in Ohio, but they had to consider a long trip with Bertha carrying the unborn baby. They planned to go soon, but could Bertha endure the three-day buggy ride and camping along the way?

The first five months of pregnancy had preceded without complications, so Rose, and other local mothers, thought the wagon travel to Ohio could be undertaken safely. This was welcome news to the newlyweds who were more than anxious to get started on their Ohio adventure.

In the spring of 1895, George and Bertha prepared to head south to George's farm and family in Weston, Ohio, some 110 miles away. As a bonus, the move would nullify any embarrassment Bertha might face in Michigan over becoming pregnant before marriage.

August heartily agreed with the move to Ohio and was pleasantly surprised to learn that George had already purchased a farm. George told August he believed the farm experience he'd gained at the Mallast farm would enable him to provide his family a good living and in fine style on his recently acquired farm in Ohio. August and Rose were both happy it was near George's mother so that Bertha would have loving support during and after her delivery, especially learning to cope with a newborn.

Rose didn't like their move to Ohio at all, but August, to placate Rose, suggested they purchase the couple a horse and wagon for their wedding gift.

August told Rose, "This will allow George and Bertha to return for annual visits."

George was very happy with this news, since he was planning on asking August for the loan of a gelding and carriage for the trip to Ohio. He happily agreed to August's proposal, but he knew trips back would be difficult to make while running a farm. He had planned on getting Bertha settled at their farm and asking his sister to stay with her while he returned the horse and wagon by himself, bringing a saddle horse with him for his return to Ohio. "This is much more straightforward," George told August.

August's proposal was much better for another reason, too, George thought. If he were traveling back to Michigan, Bertha would only have his mother and sister to lean on. Although family, they would be like strangers and Bertha would not be completely relaxed with them yet. He knew she would be okay, but he also knew it would be more stressful for her.

So it was with much sadness that Rose came to grips with George and Bertha's move from the Mallast farm to George's home in Ohio. August had purchased a used spring-loaded buggy and a horse from the village livery stable thinking it would encourage visits in future years. Rose believed their gift would allow them to visit at least once a year and wanted them to promise to return each year, but wisely, George was vague with his response. He knew leaving a farm for some period of time was not practical.

George, wanting to show his position was above that of a hired hand, offered to pay, over a reasonable period of time, half the cost of the buggy and horse. August, of course, refused, but he was impressed with George's offer.

It was a sunny May morning when the young couple began the trip south. Rose shed tears while the couple exchanged hugs with her and August and the brothers and sister. The plan was to travel about 20 miles each day, camping along the way, covering the 110 miles in about five days.

They found water and grazing for the horse along the way and the wagon did not experience any breakdowns. This was due in large part to Fred and Emil greasing the wheel bearings and replacing a nearly rusted-through spring bracket and a shaky wagon tongue.

As a welcoming gift, George's mother Nancy and sister Laura had cleaned the farmhouse that had been sitting empty for a year following George's purchase of the property. Given Bertha's condition, they didn't want her to be overwhelmed with weeks of work just to get the house livable. She was welcomed into George's family with open arms.

George's mother had given birth to eight children and was of course experienced with pregnancy and childbirth. She made an excellent midwife for the birth of their first child, a healthy baby girl born in September, 1895. Their first child, born on the George William Anthony farm in Wood County, was named Hazel.

Bertha's family, when they received her letter, were delighted with the news of a healthy baby girl.

Bertha got along very well with her mother-in-law, who moved in with the young couple after helping deliver the baby. Nancy did the household duties for the first few weeks and helped Bertha face the challenges of caring for her firstborn.

Nancy gave her some pointers on breast-feeding and Hazel was none the worse for wear; she heartily developed her lungs, especially in the evenings and at nighttime. Bertha had little spare time after her mother-in-law moved back to her own home, and the days flew by.

George's stepfather, William, had essentially vacated the farmland after George purchased it in early 1894, so when George arrived in the spring of 1895, it needed restocking and planting. Needless to say, the happy, ambitious newlywed hit the ground running. As the months passed, George kept very busy with the farm.

He immediately decided he would plant 10 acres of corn, which would give him some cash in the late fall. He would need a draft horse, plow, drag, and corn planter. He appealed to his stepfather, who loaned him his equipment for the first season. Since George was only planting 10 acres, he could phase his planting in with George's use of the equipment.

They also needed a few chickens for eggs and Sunday dinners and a milk cow for their daily needs. They would need to buy most of their other food items since the farm was in a startup mode.

George was able to purchase a cow and some chickens and a rooster from William, who was mildly amused by George's nearly frantic efforts to get everything going at once.

George cultivated another 10 acres later in the year and planted winter wheat for harvest next summer. The grain would be sold to a Bowling Green mill.

George felt a sigh of relief when the first snowflakes touched down in mid-November. He had his first winter wheat planted and ample hay in the barn for his two horses, one a draft horse he had recently purchased for plowing and another, the gelding August had given them. The gelding and carriage gift was really appreciated by the couple, since they were essential for travel to Weston for supplies and church on Sundays. He had also bought a second milk cow to assure a steady milk supply when the first went dry; they would use the extra milk to make cheese for themselves and to sell locally. They had chickens and turkeys, which he would raise and sell to help with next year's income.

George also decided, based on his Mallast farm experience, to raise some hogs. They didn't take too much care, and they reproduced at a rapid rate. He purchased two sows and a good boar for breeding so he expected a couple broods of piglets in the spring. He also purchased two calves, which he would hay-feed over the winter and turn out in a five-acre, split-log fenced field for the summer. In the late fall, after summer grazing to fatten them up, he would sell them to a meat market in Bowling Green.

Upon their arrival in 1895, he also immediately planted a large vegetable garden with an abundance of potatoes and beans, hoping to beat the autumn frost. They did beat the frost, and the garden harvest helped tide them through the winter and into the following year.

George felt comfortable and satisfied with their progress, to the delight of his mother and stepfather. He was especially anxious to prove to the Mallasts that he would be a successful farmer who could provide for his family in grand style.

George worked hard and long hours while Bertha was busy with her new duties of wife, cook, housekeeper, and new mother. Bertha was very happy for George and was proud of his progress with the farm, but to her dismay, she found she greatly missed her close-knit family on Lake St. Clair.

A year passed rapidly, but they could not find time to make the lengthy trip back to the Mallast farm. The farm required attention every day with milking and caring for the animals and poultry. The farmland was located in the large lowlands in upper Ohio, called the Black Swamp. The swamp was gradually drained by the settling farmers during the early 1800s. The exposed rich soil was excellent for growing crops and providing ample hay for winter livestock feed. They made their monthly mortgage payments on time and were even able to put some money aside for a rainy day.

George, like his father, was ambitious and a risk taker, so in 1896, when he heard a farm property in the adjacent county might be available at a relatively low price, he was interested. George was told the land was owned by a widow, who lived in Milton Center, a village a few miles to the south.

He paid her a visit soon after to discuss the property. It was about the same size as his Weston farm, 36 acres, but had an additional feature that was a real bonus for a farmer: a small stream on the western border, Beaver Creek, that would provide water for the cattle and horses. In case of a dry summer, it could provide water for their future large garden, although hauling the water from the creek would be labor intensive and time consuming.

George perceived that the widow, Margett Greeley, and the other heirs were anxious to sell, but he found in discussion that she owned only a half interest in the land.

They discussed a sale price of around $500.00, which George knew was a good bargain. With this as a talking point, he ventured forth to talk to the couple who owned the other half interest. They also lived in Milton Center.

He thought the discussion went reasonably well and thought there was a chance he could get the property, but he knew he would not be content with only a lateral transfer from one 37-acre farm to another of nearly equal size, even with Beaver Creek as a bonus.

He discussed the situation with Bertha and they decided to take a buggy ride to the Beaver Creek land. They waited for a sunny summer day, arranged for George's mother to stay with baby Hazel, and then headed west for the Henry County property.

They covered the five miles comfortably in a couple of hours and were thankful for the cooling breeze generated by the trotting horse and a prevailing western wind.

As they walked the land, George envisioned crops growing in the now-dormant fields. They especially wanted to look at the creek, both having spent time on the lake in Michigan.

They were both satisfied with the flat land. What's more, the creek, although small, was appealing.

Beaver Creek was bordered by a good stand of trees on both sides, as far as the eye could see, as it wound its way through the adjacent fields.

"The water looks pretty clear and the trees would provide a good source of firewood," George said to Bertha. "There's surprisingly a good current so we must be quite elevated above its destination river, the Maumee. That's good to be high and dry during the flooding spring season," George continued.

He observed the natural flood plain which ran about 100 feet on the farm side of the creek with the fields about 15 feet above the creek.

"Also good for watering livestock," he said, liking what he saw and giving Bertha a subtle sales pitch. "Also, there may be some fish swimming upstream in the spring to spawn. I could spear some — they would make tasty meals and nice diversion to our farm meals."

They especially liked the thought of living on a property with a flowing steam.

"It looks deep enough in spots to swim," George said. "If not," he ambitiously added, "I can dig out an adjacent small area by horse and draw bucket, to about four- or five-foot depth, then open it to the stream. Maybe build a damn across the small creek to build up water depth. We could make our own swimming pool."

George quickly had second thoughts and said to himself, "Another unrealistic idea — hope Bertha doesn't take me up on this one."

"Right," thought Bertha to herself, careful not to say it out loud. "In your spare time."

They thought it might be deep enough for a cooling dunk in the water even now but probably too shallow to swim. They were tempted to test the water but then decided against it. They didn't have suits with them and an au natural dunk might be within sight of a fairly close neighboring farm to the north.

"At least," Bertha said, "it would be a nice diversion for Hazel in later years."

George took special notice of the adjacent farms, one to the south and one to the north. He decided to return to see if either farmer would consider selling or renting. He didn't want to stop today with Bertha; he felt he would be more formidable visiting on his own to discuss the business of buying or renting.

Thus they proceeded back home to their Weston farm, both having a good feeling about the Henry County property. They had accomplished their immediate goal of looking over the land. Their walk over the vacant fields didn't go unnoticed by the adjacent farmers, who were ever curious of visitors in their rural farming area.

They liked what they saw and George decided to negotiate with the owners in Milton Center, letting them know he would only buy if he could also purchase adjacent property to gain a larger farm. This helped persuade them to lower their asking price, and they shook hands on an agreed sale price of $450.00 for each half interest, while George emphasized again that the sale was contingent on his being able to purchase adjacent land. But he was delighted. He remembered his father buying 80 acres for $4,000.00 so $900.00 for 37 acres was a great buy. "Now to see if an adjacent farmer might consider selling," he said to Bertha.

The adjacent farmers were a bit surprised when George showed up during the following week to inquire about any interest in selling. Each of the farmers had noticed the couple walking the fields a few weeks ago and suspected they might be interested in buying the vacant farm land, but they didn't think they were interested in any other property in the area.

George was most interested in the two adjacent farms on the same side of the road. He found the owner of the south farm was at least curious. The owner said he would think about it but also told George he was not the sole owner.

"I've got a partner in this, and I need to talk with my partner, Bob Wenderson, about your interest in buying. I'll consider selling," he told George, "but I need Bob's concurrence and you will have to meet our price."

He suggested George return in about a week or so while they considered his offer to buy.

George recognized the owners had the upper hand in negotiating a possible sale price, so he expected the worst when he returned.

William Singer's farm had 35 acres, a house, and a barn, along with other outbuildings, whereas the adjacent property he was negotiating to buy did not have buildings or even cleared fields. George expected the working farm would command a much higher price than the adjoining vacant property, but he was hopeful that Mr. Singer and his co-owner wouldn't be too unreasonable.

George's hopes disappeared when Mr. Singer said they wanted $2,000.00 to sell. This was much higher than the $900.00 for the same acreage George could purchase, but then again, that acreage was without a house or barn, and the fields were not cleared of brush, saplings, or some inconveniently located trees.

Mr. Singer's farm, George reasoned, did have a house, barn, outbuildings, and fields under cultivation. And there were farm animals — four cows and a couple of plow horses and associated equipment — that George thought could be negotiated into the purchase.

George was a good negotiator. He said he would think about it and return within a week if he were still interested. He visited the northern adjacent farm that day, which he hoped would not go unnoticed by Mr. Singer.

"This visit should soften Singer's asking price," George told his steed.

George did return after a week had passed and asked if he and Wenderson would accept $1,750.00.

The farmer, who had purposely started high, had rearranged with Wenderson on an acceptable sale price. George's offer was within the selling range they'd agreed upon. "All right George, we'll accept your offer of $1,750.00."

The delighted George returned home at a gallop to tell Bertha the good news.

"They agreed on $1,750.00," he told his wife, "but he wants to be paid in full at signing — no land contract with time payments to the owner."

Now George had to see if he could put the whole deal together. He would need a buyer for his Weston County farm, and although he had $600.00 plus equity in the Weston farm, this would not even come close to the $2,650.00 needed to swing the deal, i.e., $900.00 to the Milton Center owners and $1,750.00 to Singer and Wenderson. He needed to find both a lender who would accept his mortgage for the pieced together 71-acre Henry County farm and, of equal importance, a buyer for the 37-acre Wood County farm. He was hopeful they would at least break even with that sale.

George made his wish to sell the 37-acre Weston farm known at the small saloon in Weston and also placed newspaper advertisements in the Putnam County Sentinel and the Wood County Sentinel.

To his pleasant surprise, a prospective buyer emerged soon after and they agreed on a break-even price of $1,800.00.

Mr. Walters wanted all animals and equipment and George, anxious to sell, agreed to sell lock, stock, and barrel. So in August of 1896, George sold his first farm after a little more than one year on the property. He was delighted, but now he had to line up a lender for at least $1,000.00 to buy the farm in adjacent Henry County. If he could not, he would have to appeal again to his ailing stepfather for help, and maybe even to his retired grandfather, William Anthony.

George wrote to the Mallasts explaining their recent sale and trying to be as matter-of-fact as possible, so as not to alarm the in-laws. The Mallast's return letter did contain some reservations at George's "rash" move, having just spent one year on the farm. But it also contained some happy news. Bertha's sister Emilie was married in April to a John Bobcean, whose family migrated from Mechlenburg, Germany. The honeymooners were also treated to a night at the Avery House, following the wedding by Pastor Gundert and a party at the hotel. They were now farming about 20 mile north of their lake farm.

George and Bertha moved in with his mother after the Weston farm was sold. Just before doing so, he experienced yet another loss as his stepfather, William Houston, died that same month. Nancy mourned the loss of her second husband but welcomed the young family moving in with her. The hustle and bustle of the young couple with an infant helped her deal with William's death.

George proceeded to complete arrangements to purchase the three parcels, which together would make a new 71-acre farm. The properties were about five miles west of Weston, in Henry County.

The winter season, with no farming for George, allowed for a lot of leisure time and ample time to talk with prospective lenders, as well as other activities. So George was not too surprised when Bertha announced in late winter that she was expecting another baby. George and his mother were both delighted. George proudly wrote a letter to the Mallasts with the good news and apologized for not being able to visit, but proudly described their negotiations and seeking backing to purchase a bigger farm.

George was able to find a lender, who of course wanted George and Bertha to furnish a mortgage, putting both parcels on the document. Mr. C. H. Devine of Bowling Green felt comfortable loaning George and Bertha $2,000.00 with a signed note that put the entire 71 acres in a mortgage as security. So it was in March, 1897, that all three deeds were conveyed to George and Bertha and one mortgage was signed and delivered.

In less than eight months, George had sold his Weston farm, paid off the Weston mortgage, and consummated a complicated purchase of three parcels to feed his ambitious drive for a bigger farm. They were going from 37 acres to a combined 71 acres, quite an accomplishment for the young hired hand who had worked on his wife's parent's farm. August and company would surely be impressed. George knew he could now really hold his head high, and he had another child on the way to boot. Life was good!

Bertha gave birth to a healthy baby boy later that year. They wanted a distinctive name for their first son and settled on Parme. Hazel, two years old, now had a brother to play with and someone to share attention with. George had the farm working nicely, and Bertha was kept busy caring for her young family. She had thought there would be leisurely picnics by the creek, but she found that Hazel and baby Parme didn't lend themselves to leisurely picnics or to leisurely afternoons. She enjoyed social time at Sunday Church, but that was about it, with occasional visits by George's mother or sister Laura.

George and Bertha were very busy and didn't have much leisure time to write, but in 1899, George wrote to Bertha's brother Emil. He told Emil he considered him to be practically a brother to him. He also proudly wrote that another child, their third, was on the way! He knew Emil would announce the good news to his parents and siblings. He then proceeded to report their progress on the Henry County farm, knowing Emil would be very interested. George delighted in telling Emil of their good corn harvest and bragged that, "A hired hand and I shucked a record 600 bushels of corn in two days."

With crop rotation in mind, George told Emil he had no wheat that year but had planted 20 acres of winter wheat for next year's harvest. George's decision to raise pigs also was a good one, since he proudly wrote Emil that he had sold $175.00 of hogs and was fattening 15 more.

Things were going so well, he wrote Emil, that they had decided, after two years in Henry County, to build a new house. It would be back quite a ways from the County Line Road, on the edge of the Beaver Creek flood plain. Their view would look down on the tree-lined creek about 200 feet away and into a shallow valley with surrounding farm fields.

George's hired hand would live in the original farmhouse and keep an eye on the barn, poultry coops, and animals.

George was happy as a clam as a new century approached and baby Darel was born, but poor Bertha didn't have a breather. Although she was delighted with their happy and healthy family, George sensed she didn't share his euphoria.

After the initial excitement and adjustment of living with George in Ohio, busy with housework and infants to look after, Bertha found she missed the Mallast farm and the nearby lake and marsh. More importantly, she missed her family, especially her mother. Letters were exchanged haphazardly, and as the years flew by, Bertha began to miss her family more and more, especially her dear mother Rose. She kept her feelings to herself for a long time, but she finally decided to discuss them with George in mid-1900.

George could understand her feelings and was sympathetic to his young bride's longing for home, but this did cause a dilemma for him. His family would be disappointed if he left Ohio. Besides, he and Bertha had a new house and a good farm, but eventually Bertha prevailed with her unwavering position. After a few months, she wore George down and they decided to return to the Mallast farm area in Michigan. Although somewhat disappointed, George was not too resistant to return to the Mallast farm, especially since his experiences were so fondly remembered. George vividly recalled the good times on the farm with the Mallast's sons and with Bertha and all the great recreation and diversion during the summers and falls on

Lake St. Clair. Besides, he got along very well with the brothers, especially his favorite, Emil.

George felt comfortable with this decision, since his mother, like before, would not be left alone in Ohio. Nancy, being a social person, was courted and married Henry Bartel of McClure in Henry County. She had moved to McClure, about six miles away, to live with Henry and his teenage son. So she had a husband, a stepson, three sons on the 80-acre Weston farm, and a married daughter with two children. George concluded she would not be lonesome at all.

RETURN TO MICHIGAN

Rose was overwhelmed with joy when she read the letter in late 1900 announcing their intent to return. Bertha explained that George loved his farm and would need to find a suitable buyer. Importantly, she explained that they were not going to sell at all costs.

George reluctantly broke the news to his mother Nancy, who was saddened but understood Bertha's homesick feelings.

The family's decision to return to Michigan was likewise greeted with disappointment but accepted by George's four siblings.

George ran three newspaper advertisements; the Wood County Sentinel, the Henry County Signal, and the Putnam County Sentinel. His farm was about in the center of the three county seats. Near the end of winter in 1901, a prospective buyer, Mr. Stretchberry, showed up at the door. He was quite interested in the farm and they agreed on a purchase price of

$3,750.00 without the farm equipment and animals. The sale was to be completed in September, 1901.

The mortgage to Mr. Divine was paid and cancelled the same September day, so George now planned an auction to be held in October.

The auction took place with many items bid for and purchased by the new farm owner, Foster Stretchberry, including horses, cows, pigs, wagons, farm planting and harvest equipment, and miscellaneous items such as hand tools and kitchen items.

The new farm owner also purchased a drag, two cultivators, a horse-driven hay rake, a binder, nearly all of George's shoats, sows, and piglets, plus a horse-drawn sleigh, fork, hoes, mole trap, chain, barrel, butter churn, jars, grind stone, harness, stove, and bedstead. Mr. Stretchberry was getting ready for farming, and before the auction he made an agreement to purchase the two milk cows, a steer, a colt, and two draft horses.

George and Bertha kept very good records of money matters and they reviewed the day's sales and summed the money received. Many smaller items sold for nickels and dimes, but some such as the shoals, sows, and pigs went for nearly $50.00. The total for the auction was $254.00 in addition to the cows and horses — a tidy sum to add to their savings for a farm purchase in Michigan.

George and Bertha now had quite a profit: $1,100.00, over two years' full pay at the generous industrial labor rate of $2.00 per day in 1901. The land sale, auction sale, and savings from five years of farming would probably be enough make a significant down payment on a farm in Michigan, hopefully in the vicinity of Bertha's parents. This thought made their move back to Michigan even more appealing.

With their affairs settled, George and Bertha took their gelding and sprung carriage and headed north to Michigan, this time devoid of Fred and Emil's maintenance efforts. Of course, they now had three additional travelers on the return trip, six-year-old Hazel, four-year-old Parme, and two-year-old Darel.

They deposited their money in a Bowling Green Bank for bank transfer to Michigan. He did not want to be on the road, camping overnight, with a large amount of cash.

"Your parents will be impressed," George said to Bertha as they crossed the Michigan-Ohio line.

The travel again took five days, but the early fall was kind. Despite a few rain squalls, they stayed relatively dry with the canvas canopy top firmly in place. The roads were passable and camping was fun. George did not push, but kept the horse at a comfortable, even pace of about four miles per hour. This helped the young children endure the 110-mile trek north.

All told, it was a big adventure for his young children. Two-year-old Darel slept a lot, frequently rocked to sleep in his makeshift bed by the swaying and rocking of the horse-drawn carriage. They arrived at the Mallast farm no worse for the wear and in good spirits. George's horse, the gelding, was none the worse for wear either, and the carriage held up well.

August and Rose were delighted when they saw George, Bertha, and the children, whom they had never met, pull into their yard. Hazel and Parme scampered out of the wagon and into their grandparents' arms, and George lifted Darel up to see his grandparents for the first time. They had come home to the farm and to the grandparents they had heard so much about from their mother and father. It was also fairly obvious to both August and Rose that another Anthony was on the way.

George and Bertha were given the loan of the large upstairs bedroom while brothers Fred and Emil moved to George's old room in the barn.

Fred and Emil were also delighted at the return of their good friend and sister, so the use of their bedroom, for a while anyway, was perfectly all right.

The twins, Emilie and Adolphine, were both married, as were Bertha's two oldest brothers, Rudolph and Adolph. This allowed a downstairs bedroom for Hazel and Parme while Darel slept upstairs with George and Bertha.

The wanderers had returned triumphant, in good health, with three healthy children and a high degree of optimism based on their successful six years in Ohio. And with a handsome profit to enable them to buy a farm, hopefully close to Bertha's homestead.

The Mallasts were visibly happy and impressed. Life was indeed good!

Acknowledgments

Many people helped furnish information and materials in my quest to make *Mallast* as authentic as possible. I was fortunate to have a firsthand information source for details of Mallast family farm life in the early 1900s.

My aunt Hilda Anthony, granddaughter of August and Rose Mallast, at 102 years of age, sharp as a tack, living on her own, spent many hours in discussions with me describing her weekend stays at the lake farm with her grandparents. She was to be co-author of *Mallast*, since much of the historical 1900s'-era material was provided by her during our many discussions. However, God had another plan and at 103 years of age, she passed on.

My special thanks also goes to my cousin Margie (Anthony) Harris, who graciously and unselfishly shared her volumes of genealogy work on the Mallast and Anthony families and participated in many discussions regarding our ancestors.

Finally, a sincere thank you to the people and organizations listed below for their assistance in furnishing or obtaining information used in the writing of this historical novel.

Michelle Johnson, Macomb County (Michigan) Recorder of Deeds staff, guided me through early records, allowing a history of the Mallast farmland beginning in 1805 plus Mallast property purchases in the late 1800s.

Dr. (Ed.D.) Raymond Phil Groh Jr., archivist of the Mt. Clemens Zion United Church of Christ, formerly the German Evangelical Protestant Church attended by the Mallast family in the late 1800s, furnished many church records dating back to the 1890s as well as provided his rich perspective of life in Europe and Michigan in the nineteenth century.

Cynthia Bieniek, archivist of the Arthur M. Woodford History Center of the St. Clair Shores (Michigan) Public Library, was instrumental in suggesting I include 1890s'-era Detroit establishments and history. She furnished names and storyline suggestions that are incorporated in this work. She also steered me to useful sources of rich marine history for the Port of Detroit.

Captain John Sarns, Great Lakes freighter captain and author of the book *Always on Duty*, led me further into sources of marine history of the Great Lakes. He worked for the Oglebay Norton line and is currently semi-retired.

Joel Stone, curator of the Detroit Historical Society, furnished information on grain shipping from the Port of Detroit in the 1800s.

John Polacsek, a very knowledgeable Great Lakes historian, identified schooners active in the 1800s and also gave me sources of early Detroit and marine information of that era.

The Detroit Public Library maintained a helpful microfilm archive of the *Detroit Free Press* and, most importantly, an online database of short synopses of newspaper articles dating back to the pre-1850s.

Mt. Clemens Public Library made available their Genealogy Room material.

The staff of the Bloomfield Hills Family History Center (Church of Jesus Christ of Latter-day Saints) helped in locating some 1860s'-era Prussian military records.

Ms. Lioba Scheermann of the Bundesarchiv-Militarchiv of Germany helped in attempting to locate Prussian military records of the 1800s.

The Evangelisches Zentralarchiv in Berlin helped in the search for church and military records.

Ms. Irene Szlachtowicz, managing owner of Miller Brothers Dairy store in Mt. Clemens, was born in Germany and graciously helped compose and translate a number of letters to and from the above German organizations.

Duane Mallast, a great-grandson of August and Rose, furnished documents related to his grandfather, Adolph Mallast. These included a copy of Adolph's 1879 Confirmation in Rogasen, Prussia.

Gary Mallast, great-grandson of August and Rose and grandson of Rudolph Mallast, furnished historic family photographs, including Rudolph's blacksmith shop, and a copy of Rudolph's 1886 marriage certificate. Gary and his brother-in-law, Joe Robinson, furnished other historic family information as well. Gary is author of the book *The 1938–'39 Ford Book for Passenger Cars*.

Steve Semrau advised me on the French-German contested area of Alsace-Lorraine with information enriched by his heritage and firsthand knowledge.

Steve Loveland, staff member of the Methodist Church in Mt. Clemens, assisted me in searching for Anthony family facts.

Marie Ling McDougal, author of the book Mt. *Clemens Bath City U.S.A.*, also wrote the book entitled *Harrison Township*, which I used frequently as a reference for other 1880s'-era families in the Lake St. Clair farm area.

The Recorder of Deeds staff of Ohio Henry County, Sara Myles (recorder), Christy Prigge, and Deb Silveus; and the Recorder of Deeds staff of Wood County, Julie Baumgardner, all helped me trace the moves of my grandfather Anthony's family during his youth and early married life.

The Probate Courts of Ohio staff, Lisa Miller of Crawford County, Kimberly Bischoff of Henry County, and Kim Rothenbuhler of Wood County, all expeditiously answered my numerous letter requests for birth and death records of the Henry Anthony family of Ohio in the 1860–1881 time period.

Marlena Ballinger, managing editor of the *Putnam County Sentinel*, furnished archive information of the Anthony fire.

The Wood County Chapter of the Ohio Genealogy Society furnished copies of requested obituaries.

The Clinton Grove Cemetery of Mt. Clemens maintained family records and the Stockman Cemetery of Henry County continues to provide upkeep of the 1880 Henry Anthony gravestone and base.

The database managers of Ancestry.com and information sources available on the Internet.

Last, thank you to the book publishing staff of Jenkins Group of Traverse City, Michigan, for their cooperation in publishing this book.

This was an interesting and widely varied search that did not produce all the answers I sought but that did establish many facts, coupled with family lore, from which I was able to weave a story.

Rationale

When writing a historical novel based on family history
that takes place over one hundred years ago, it is practically
impossible to glean all the significant events of a family's life
during that period. Despite the fact that I am a great-grandson
of the main characters and have the benefit of inherited family
lore, as well as extensive information extracted from public and
church records, I still needed to make two major assumptions in
Mallast.

Assumption one: the Mallasts
were tenant farmers in Europe

Farming was the major occupation in Europe in the year 1860
with properties owned by noblemen and rented to tenants who
worked the land and managed the farm. The word "laborer" is
vastly predominant in immigration ship manifests with very few
individuals shown as "farmer laborer." The word "laborer" is also
used in U.S. Census reports of 1880 and 1900 to clearly identify
the occupation of "working on a farm."

Such was the case for the family head, August Mallast, on
the manifest from his immigration ship. In the 1900 U.S. Census

report, August is listed as "farmer" while the boys at home are listed as "laborers." (The migration occurred in 1882, but most of the 1890 U.S. Census reports were destroyed by fire.)

Further, it would take prior farm management experience to successfully begin farming in Michigan during the difficult farm period of 1882–1900. This experience, of course, had to have occurred in Prussia.

ASSUMPTION TWO: THE MALLAST FAMILY BEGAN FARMING SOON AFTER THEIR ARRIVAL IN MICHIGAN

The Mallast family arrived in the summer of 1882. The lake farm was deeded to August and Rose Mallast in 1893 but a deed of adjacent property states that a son (Adolph) fenced the property next to the Mallast farm in 1890, no doubt for additional farmland use. This shows that the Mallasts were farming on the lake farm prior to actually owning the farm.

I was told by a senior farm owner that even in the 1920s–'30s, the practice was to rent out a farm and, if the renters liked the property and vice versa, to offer them the option of buying it. This is consistent with the story I tell.

OTHER RATIONALE:

1. Property Deeds and Mortgages

Property deeds and mortgages are used to identify locations of the Mallast farm and various farm neighbors. Such is also the case for the various Anthony farms in Ohio owned by Henry,

George, and Nancy (Anthony) Houston. Also, deeds and mortgages are used to identify the location of Rudolph's Mt. Clemens workplace and his subsequent business as well as the Perrysburg, Ohio, business of William M. Houston.

2. Military and Rank

August told a grandson he served in four wars in Europe. The decade preceding the Mallast migration saw three wars fought by Prussia: 1864 Denmark, 1866 Austria, and 1870–'71 France. The fourth war could have been an 1850 conflict with Denmark or the unsuccessful uprising in that same period, although August would have been only fifteen years old.

A letter written by August's son-in-law contains reference to "the major." My attempt to substantiate this by viewing microfilm of the Rogasen military church records of 1864–1870 was unsuccessful. I then sponsored a search of the existing Prussian military records, despite the fact that most records were destroyed in bombings during the Second World War. This search was unsuccessful as well.

A few Nawish village military were contained in the microfilm, substantiating that the surrounding village personnel were part of the Rogasen Infantry Regiment.

I have not specified a rank for August but have placed him in the three Prussian wars of the 1860s, referencing significant battles in each for effect.

3. Birthplace and Europe Farm Location

The birthplaces are consistently recorded on all the family cemetery records and most Michigan church records as

Werdum, Prussia; a village three miles west of the town of Rogasen. However, a copy of Bertha's birth record and a copy of the migration ticket receipt lists Nawish as the "home village," which is also three miles from Rogasen but to the south. A copy of a son's (Adolph's) 1879 Confirmation record lists the church as being in Rogasen. Because of the consistency and preponderance of U.S. records, the farm is placed in Werdum, Prussia. Perhaps Rosina returned to her mother's house for childbirth, a fairly common practice in Germany for that time period according to a German church archivist.

4. Migration in Steerage Class

My quest for substantiation of steerage for all Mallast family members was successful. The name of each family member was found in the steerage listings of the two migration ships the Mallasts used in migrating from Germany to the United States. Steerage was the economy class of the time.

5. Bertha's Mother-in-Law

The story evolves into a marriage between the youngest Mallast child, Bertha, and a young Ohioan. The husband's family history is interwoven to depict the hardships of farm life and the tragedies he endured during his formative years on two farms in Ohio.

The mother-in-law, Nancy Anthony, is recorded as giving birth to seven children in a 1900 Census record. However, Ohio birth records, Census reports, and a cemetery headstone prove there were eight children. Perhaps Nancy blocked a child out because of a traumatic tragedy. In the same Census document, she declares correctly that five of the children were living. For the record, the eight children were Laura, Joe, Charles, George, Mary, Flora, Rolland, and Otto. (Two additional names have been used in various places, Harriet and Henry Jr., but records prove that Harriet is Laura Della and Henry Jr. is Rolland.)

6. Names

Names of businesses, hotels, restaurants, saloons, train lines, and lake schooners are valid but not necessarily all used by the Mallast family.

7. Events Moved in Time

The Villerot family moved next to the Mallast farm in 1890 but I decided to use the French family and sons to interact with the Mallasts eight years earlier. The Villerots bring in the French farming element common in the lake area and enrich the Mallast's farm experiences.

Although sunk at a later date than 1882, a report of the sinking of the ship *Geiser* contains insight into the use of life-saving equipment aboard large ocean-going passenger ships of the time, including the cork life belt (predecessor to the life vest) and the lifeboat.

The ships *F.G. Fort* and *Gulf of Panama* were lost at dates that are not consistent with the story but that did occur in the late 1800s. The sinking of the *F. G. Fort* depicts the potential hazards of crewing on Great Lakes ships in that era. The *Gulf of Panama* shipwreck depicts the risks associated with shipping grain across the Atlantic Ocean and the corresponding loss of profits.

ABOUT THE AUTHOR

Bob Prevost is a great-grandson of the Mallast family parents, privy to family lore and genealogy work accomplished over years by a dear cousin, Margie Harris. Family lore was primarily obtained from a mentally-sharp and physically-able 102-year-old aunt, *Hilda Anthony,* who knew most of the Mallast family. Other information was passed down over the years by uncles and especially my mother, a granddaughter of the Mallast's.

Bob is a graduate engineer, holding a bachelor's degree from the University of Detroit and a masters degree in engineering from the University of Michigan. He worked for Goodyear Aircraft following graduation and subsequently served three years in the United States Air Force as an Aircraft Maintenance Officer. He joined General Motors Corporation, where he held numerous engineering and management positions over the past decades.

He was raised on a farm in Michigan during the mid-1900s and experienced firsthand the numerous farm jobs and the tough financial times *in* the post depression *era* of the 1930s and 40s.

Bob and his wife, Jocelyn, reside on the property described in the book as the "marshland peninsula", in the vicinity of the Mallast farm property. They have raised their three children at that same lakeside location. Their daughters, Dr. Paula Prevost-Blank and Dr. Kristen Cares, are medical doctors (MDs) while their son, Jim, is a Registered Professional Civil Engineer and principal in Barr and Prevost, a civil engineering company in Ohio.